Drunk
ON A THUG'S
LOVE
Skyy & Remy

A Novel By

BLAKE KARRINGTON

SYNOPSIS

Skyy Pearson is tired of being controlled and hurt by those she loves. After losing her mother to a drug overdose and living on the streets, Skyy finds solace in Malachi, the man who took her in and made her his girl. But being the girlfriend of such a pretentious, controlling and lying man can quickly take it's toll. At 23 years old, Skyy has finally had enough of the bullshit and is ready to do things for herself. Sometimes starting over isn't easy but when she meets Remy, she realizes that starting over can mean so much more.

Remy Deveaux isn't thinking about love. When his fiancé and child died, so did his heart. All that's out there for him is money and bitches. He's got a good thing going and has plenty of women lining up to do whatever he wants but Skyy proves to be the exception to that.

What starts off as a little freaky fun turns into something that neither one expects. But of course, when something good comes along, a lot of bad tends to follow. Will Skyy and Remys relationship be strong enough to survive their issues or would it be best for both of them to just let go?

PROLOGUE

"Ma! Ms. Erma said you got your music too loud and if you don't turn it down, she's gonna call the front office and complain." I yelled walking into the house from school. " And I need $10 so that I can go on this field trip on Friday too."

I walked over to cut the music down mama had blasting on the stereo.

Why the hell she had this music so damn loud? She know Ms. Erma complains about every little thing. I thought to myself.

I walked through our two-bedroom apartment looking to see where my mama was at. I needed her to sign this permission slip and to give me the money before it was too late. I was trying to go on a field trip to the Wax museum at the end of the week and I knew she had gotten her check today.

Mama had got a check from social security every month for me since my daddy had passed away. He was an army war veteran that was killed when I was like ten years old. Me and Mama both knew that It was going to stop soon though because I was going to be eighteen in another year. I had always been trying to save a little bit of money from time to time but, mama had a heavy drug problem a while back, mainly from his death and a lot of times that check would be gone within a day. She had recently got it together and was clean. Also she had started back working and things were looking up for the first time in a while.

"Ma! Where you at?" I yelled not seeing her in the living room or my room.

Knowing my mama, she was probably in her room binge watching Law & Order SVU and eating God knows what type of junk food. It was her day off and that's all she ever did to relax.

I shook my head at the mess in the apartment. I swear sometimes she was more like my child than my mama with the way I had to fuss at her about keeping things clean.

I walked towards her bedroom and could hear Benson and Stablers voices coming through the TV.

"You know Ms. Erma mad right now for you blasting that mu—"

My body froze the second I stepped into her room.

"M—m—mama?" I whispered, sensing something wasn't right.

She was face down in the middle of the bed, her right arm dangling from the side of the mattress. My eyes darted around the room, trying to figure out what was going on. When they finally settled on the white powder and needle on the nightstand by her bed my entire soul left my body.

"No! No! No!" I screamed running towards her and turning her limp frame over.

I cradled my mama in my arms while checking to see if she was still breathing. Her skin was cold and wet. Her face was pale and void of any kind of emotion. Panicking, I laid her body back down on the bed and started performing CPR. Tears continued to fall from my eyes as I begged God to help me save her life again.

"Come on mama get up!" I yelled while pressing hard on her chest.

This wasn't her first time OD'n. I've had to revive my mother on more than one occasion. She was so close to dying the last time that it took weeks for her to get better. That brush with death scared her so much that she decided to get clean. Mama promised that I would never find her like that again, yet here I was.

I pumped and pumped for so long, my arms and hands began to hurt.

My effort to try and save her wasn't working. She still wasn't moving.

I thought about calling 911 but the last time the police came the state took me away from her and she had to fight like hell to get me back. I ran to the bathroom and filled the mop bucket up with cold water from the tub. I had seen in this movie where the girl splashed cold water on her best friend to bring her out of a coma. I dashed mamas now colorless body with the nearly freezing water and it did nothing. Deep down inside I knew that she was really gone this time.

My mama was dead.

I slumped to the floor and began to cry. I hadn't told her how much I loved her in a long time. I was in my teenage years and it seemed like we argued about everything. Mainly at how much I resented the fact that I had to be the adult. My emotions shifted from sorrow to anger.

She had promised me she was going to be clean! She promised! She said that she would never let them take me away from her again.

How did I not know that she was using again?

"Mama." I sniffed, now holding her lifeless body in my arms.

I sat rocking and crying for hours while stroking her face. She was all I had. My father was gone *and now* my mother had left me. I was really all alone. I knew the state was going to take me before the morgue could even get her body. Who would bury her if that happened? All we had was each other. I thought about the fuck nigga Dre, who would come and spend the night with her from time the time but they weren't serious. He was probably the reason she was back on this shit.

I wiped my eyes and looked around. What would I do? Where would I go? I wasn't going back into the system. I couldn't go back into foster care. I wouldn't wish that shit on my worst enemy. It was the worst place to put a kid. I knew my mama wouldn't want that for me.

I looked around and saw her purse sitting in the corner. Letting her go, I walked over to it and opened it to see if she had cashed her paycheck and the check from Social Security. Counting the money, I saw it was a little over $500. She must have spent the rest on drugs because I knew there were still some bills that she hadn't paid.

I put the money in my pocket and went into my room to grab the small duffle bag that I got when I was a cheerleader at school a few years ago. I threw a bunch of clean clothes, some underwear, and a few pictures of me and mama inside before throwing it over my shoulder. I knew it was only a matter of time before someone found out that she had died and there was no way I could take care of the bills and stuff by myself.

I walked back into her room and looked at my mama laying on the bed like she was sleeping. I wanted to fall out and cry all over again, but I needed to go, otherwise I would never have the nerve to leave. Walking over to her, I kissed her cheek.

"I love you mama." I whispered.

I turned and walked out of the room and headed to the front door saying a silent prayer that God looked after my mama in heaven.

SKYY

"Skyy wake up!"

"Huh?"

"Wake up. Damn you been tossing and turning and talking all kinds of crazy shit. I can't get any sleep."

I sat up turning to look at him like he was out of his damn mind.

"Excuse the hell out of me for having a nightmare." I said sarcastically.

"Skyy—don't start. I have to be at work in like three hours. You know I got this big case coming up. I need to get my sleep." Malachi complained.

"Okay. So go to sleep then!" I snapped.

"Well I can't if you're doing all this talking and moving all over the place," he mumbled.

"You know what?" I got out the bed putting on my house shoes and robe. "How about I just go sleep on the couch so that you can get your precious rest. Since apparently you're the only thing that matters in this damn relationship anyway."

He sighed sitting up rubbing his head in frustration or whatever it was. I didn't care.

"Skyy that's not what I meant," he said.

"Whatever Malachi." I shrugged yawning. "Clearly all you care about is you. You ain't even ask me if I was okay. You didn't ask me did I want to talk about it. Nothing. All you're concerned about is you, as always. So I'll let you sleep. Right here by yourself."

I walked out slamming the door not giving a damn and flopped down on the couch angrily. Malachi was such an asshole. Why in the hell was I even with him? His anal-retentive ass made me sick. We had been together for close to four years and everything was always about him. That's how our entire relationship had been.

I met Malachi right after I turned eighteen. I was sitting at the bus stop with only thirty-five cents to my name. I didn't have a job, I didn't have any money and I didn't have any place to go. I had gone inside this restaurant to try to get warm because it was like thirteen degrees outside in February and in Charlotte, North Carolina it could get really cold. So cold that the governor would declare a state of emergency and would shut down the whole state if he even thought it was going to snow.

The manager was being a dick and telling me that I had to buy something otherwise I couldn't be in there. Malachi overheard the ass hole's warning and quickly came to my rescue. He pretended like he was my boyfriend. I was a little weirded out by it at first but he was really sweet and I was freezing since I only had a sweatshirt and some jeans on so I went along with it.

I don't think the manager believed him because he was dressed in a suit and I was looking like I came straight out the shelter, which I had. Either way it worked and he left me alone.

We sat down and he dominated the conversation with stories about his life. I should have known then that he was narcissistic as hell. But I met him at a time where I was at my lowest. Not to just say that I was desperate, he was also really nice to me and I had never had that from a man without them first trying to get something from me.

Even though he offered, I refused to go home with him that night. He was nice, but the nigga was still a stranger at the end of the day. Needless to say, I took the money he gave to me that night before going back to the shelter and called him the next day just as he requested. I don't know why I did it but I did and he offered me a job as an assistant for him at his father's law firm. I caught plenty of looks from the other staff members and of course folks were gossiping about what I was doing with him but, I had a job. He gave me an advance in pay so I could get a hotel and some clothes.

I had never seen that much money from a job before! The most I had done was waitressing to make ends meet, so to have a job where my name was on a check and it had a comma in it for one week of work, and answering phones at that? I was excited. I was smart though. I didn't go spending my money on some expensive hotel like he thought I should. I got a cheap motel room and got my clothes from the Goodwill to wear to work. What I didn't spend, I saved.

Malachi would stop by my desk every day and bring me lunch before he would go talk to his father. We would have small talk and he would always compliment me on how I looked. He would suggest that we go out and I would always say no. I was grateful for the job and a chance to make money but I didn't want to be some glorified prostitute. I rejected him for three months straight.

Then one day I was at work and some crazy ass gunman came into the firm running from the cops. He locked himself inside with us. I was scared out of my mind. Hell everybody was. I was crying and praying to God. I didn't want to die. I was crying hard. He turned around and aimed his gun at me and my heart started racing. Malachi stepped in front of me and talked this fool down. I was looking at him like he had lost his damn mind. That was the dumbest thing I had ever seen in my life. But, he actually distracted this fool and punched his ass so hard he knocked him out. I was in shock.

I don't know why, but despite how dumb he was for putting his life at risk for me, it was something that was so sexy about it. It was like one of those trashy romance novels that some of these women read where the main male character saves the day and the damsel in distress throws herself at him. I didn't do all of that but the next time he asked me out, I did say yes. From that moment on we started dating and not long after we made it official.

After we got into a relationship, he slowly but surely started to show his true colors. He thought it would be better for me not to work with him to avoid any *unnecessary* work issues. I agreed because I knew we were the talk of the office and it wasn't that many black folks there anyway. I left the company, moved in with him, and became the typical girlfriend that didn't work. My new job was to stay home, keep the house clean, and to have dinner ready when Malachi walked through the door. It wasn't bad, but I really didn't have much of a life outside of the GED program that I had enrolled in.

I had one best friend named Tierra who couldn't stand Malachi. She thought that he was way too controlling and she was right. But even with his controlling ways I've never wanted for anything. I know that probably makes me sound weak, but I had gotten comfortable and happy with my life and not having to struggle anymore so I just learned to deal with his tendencies.

Don't get me wrong, he wasn't always a jerk. He had a really sweet side to him. And like I said, I never wanted for anything. He kept me dripping with new bags and diamonds and if I ever needed money, he had it. Granted, he would bitch every now and then about what I spent it on, but he made me happy.

Sexually he wasn't bad either. He was the first and only person I had ever given myself to so it was easy to say that. He loved to make love. He loved to dominate in the bedroom and I found it sexy. I just hated that he finished so quickly sometimes, mainly when I was riding him. Like I would just be getting a groove going and he would nut and I would be disappointed. He would make up for it though by eating me out or fucking me from the back which was my favorite position. He taught me everything I knew about sex. Well, him and Pornhub. When he would go to work, oh my ass was watching some Pornhub to get some ideas. That and to take the edge off sometimes. Overall, we had a good relationship. But tonight was just one of those nights where it wasn't good.

I heard him shuffling into the living room and turned around to see him wiping his eyes. I had to admit, he was a nice piece of man. He was six foot two and exactly 195 pounds. He took care of his body and ate healthy. He made sure of that. He was standing in front of me with just his boxers on looking like a light-skinned Ken doll with a durag. For a second, I forgot why I was mad at him.

"Babe come on back to bed," he yawned.

"I'm not really that tired anymore." I told him.

My mom had been on my brain heavy. The last couple of days I had been thinking about her so much. I hated when this happened. I could go months without crying but every now and then I would think about her and it just wouldn't stop. Today was one of those days. It had been like this all week.

"What were you dreaming about?" He asked.

"My mama." I whispered.

He nodded and came to sit down next to me.

He never really talked about her. I told him what happened when we first started dating and he would tell me that he was glad that I ran away because I was too good for that lifestyle.

Malachi grew up with a silver spoon in his mouth. His parents were both doctors and lawyers. They expected greatness of him. He wouldn't know how to survive in the ghetto. In his mind, he was better than that. When he told his mom about my background, she acted like I was a charity case. I couldn't stand that bitch. But I respected her because Malachi was her son. Even if he was a mama's boy.

He pulled me to him and hugged me, and I could feel myself starting to cry.

"I don't understand why I keep having the same dream. I keep dreaming about me walking in the house and finding her in her room." I told him.

He sat and rubbed my back listening to me and comforted me while I cried. This was the side of him that I loved. Even though he didn't know what to say, he was still there for me.

"I miss her so much." I admitted.

He nodded his head and yawned again. I sniffed wiping my eyes and felt bad. I just snapped on him and he was exhausted. He worked really hard. He had been up all night getting ready for a case. He was an attorney fresh out of law school but had been hired at one of the top firms in Charlotte. It wasn't surprising though seeing as how his father was one of the biggest attorneys in the state. The last name Jackson carries weight.

Everybody was asking us when we were going to get married, but he felt like we weren't ready. He wanted us to be together for a couple more years before we cross that bridge. He had his entire life mapped out. We were going to be in a relationship for five years and if everything was good then we would get engaged. That would take another year and then we would have our wedding. Kids? Yeah that was out of the question for at least another eight years. Yeah, my man was a little bit anal retentive, but still for the most part he made me happy.

"Why don't you go ahead and go to bed?" I suggested. "You need your rest. I'll be okay."

"Are you sure?" He asked already standing up and heading back towards the room.

"Yeah." I nodded.

"All right. Good night."

I watched him walk off as I laid down on the couch. Normally Malachi would complain about me sleeping on the couch and say that I was wearing it out that way. But tonight was just one of those nights that I didn't care. I turned on the TV and started flipping through the channels aimlessly to find something to watch but my mom was still on my mind. The guilt of how I left her that day had been with me for so long. I wanted to talk to somebody about it, but Malachi said that black people don't go to therapy. Even though his mother was a psychologist he had an issue with me going to one.

When I questioned him on it and mentioned his mother's profession, all he said was that he didn't feel like I should be telling my business to a complete stranger. He actually suggested that I talk to his mother about it if I insisted on talking to anyone about it but ain't no way in hell that would happen. She was too damn judgmental and I would cuss her ass out if she even thought about saying something negative about my mama. So instead, I just kept it to myself.

Grabbing an Afghan off the chair next to me, I curled up to get comfortable. I prayed to God that my mama was up in heaven looking down on me. Hopefully she was proud and happy. Despite everything that happened, I managed to get my GED. I wanted to go to college but after a while that goal was becoming more of a dream. But I promised myself to never fully give up on going. I just had to figure out how to fit it into Malachi's grand scheme of things. I still wanted to be able to do for myself.

I thought about texting my bestie to see if she was up but decided against it. She literally was like a sister to me. Even though her and Malachi didn't get along and he thought that she was too ghetto, she had been tight with me from the day we got our GED together. I met her in the classroom and we became instant friends. She was a lot like me; young, carefree. She really didn't have any responsibilities. She always had men around her. I couldn't blame them though, hell if I was gay I'd be on her quick. She was gorgeous, and confident. She was the type of chick that would never deal with Malachi's ways. Anytime they were around each other it was interesting. She kept her comments to herself out of respect for me. At least until we were away from him. Then she would let loose.

His dislike for her was just as strong as hers was for him. She would remind me that he couldn't keep me under lock and key. Just because he wasn't a sociable person didn't mean I would have to be. At least once a week though while he was at work, Tierra and I would go out and have a girl's day. Sometimes I would go out with her to the clubs and it would agitate the hell out of Malachi. I mainly did that when I was mad at him though. He would fuss about how it looked to people that I was going to the club with my single friend and I had a man, but damn! I was twenty-one. I still had to have a life of my own. Malachi wasn't adventurous or spontaneous at all.

We would go out for dinner once a week, or go to his parents or go to church, but other than that, I was always at the house making sure that it stayed clean, making sure that his meals were ready, or I was at the gym. I made sure to keep my figure tight because I didn't want to lose my form. If I put on a little bit of weight, he would let me know.

Maybe that's what I needed was to go out and have some fun.

Whatever it was, I had to do something because this pain was just too much to deal with.

Settling on TV One, I curled up under the Afghan, and let old reruns of Martin entertain me for a while.

I was dozing when I heard a buzzing noise coming from the other side of the room. I got up and walked over realizing it was Malachi's phone and saw Zoey's name popping up on his caller ID.

Oh I answered that shit so quick!

"Why the fuck are you calling my man at one o'clock in the morning?" I questioned.

"Um...because I need him to send me the files on the Logan case," she replied sarcastically. "Somebody's feeling insecure."

"No. Somebody's sleeping and you're interrupting our night!" I snapped. "I don't give a fuck what you need. You can wait until the morning like everybody else."

"Oh my God. Must you speak so crass?" She pushed.

"Must I kick your ass?" I fired back.

She sighed and I let her know what was up.

"Don't call his phone this late again." I warned.

I hung up the phone not even giving her an opportunity to answer. I put the phone down pissed off and walked back to the couch. The nerve of this bitch to be calling his phone this fucking late. She wasn't going to be happy until I dog walked her ass.

I knew her ass was going to say something to Malachi about it too. He better check that hoe. She was getting too comfortable.

Something told me to check his phone. I've never checked his phone before because I really didn't have a reason to. But this bitch was way too friendly and clearly she thought it was cool to call this late; work or not. And I'm not the kind of bitch that's gonna check the bitch. I'm gonna check the man. Don't get it twisted, she was gonna get hers because she knew that was my man. But he should've put a stop to that shit a long time ago.

I picked up his phone and went straight to her contact. I could see all the texts and calls and my mouth damn near hit the floor.

There was a long ass thread of text messages and calls. And a lot of them shits was after work hours when he was supposed to be at the gym or some shit.

"What the fuck?" I mumbled.

I was looking at pictures of this bitch in his phone in fucking bikinis and shit and him telling her pasty ass how good she looked.

"What are you doing?" I heard.

I jumped seeing him standing in front of me.

"The better question is, what the fuck are you doing?" I asked turning the phone to him and showing him exactly what the fuck I was looking at. "So you and this white bitch fucking around?"

"Skyy, it's almost two in the morning. Why are you going through my phone?" he questioned.

"Why are y'all talking to each other so much? Why is she sending you pics of her? Why is she calling you this late?" I rattled off. "Are you fucking this bitch or not?"

I was so close to him I was practically his second layer of skin.

"Do you have any viable proof that I'm cheating on you?" he asked with no emotion.

"I'm not on the goddamn stand Malachi!" I yelled. "I'm not one of your fucking witnesses on the stand. Now you tell me what's going on. NOW!"

He looked at me and shook his head before taking his phone out of my hand and walking back into the bedroom.

"Oh so you just gonna walk your ass the fuck off? You not gonna answer me?"

He kept walking and closed the door and I was standing there trying to figure out what the fuck just happened.

He was cheating. He was cheating on me with that bitch. Viable proof? Viable fucking proof? The shit was there! You don't entertain another bitch when you got a girlfriend! A girlfriend you've been with for almost four fucking years!

I marched back over to the couch numb and sat down. I didn't know what the fuck was happening. The one time I go look through this niggas phone and I see this shit. I couldn't even cry I was so mad. He was in bed sleeping like a baby or probably messaging her ass right now and I was out on the couch? This shit was so fucking surreal.

I tried to focus on TV but, this shit was on my brain heavy. I couldn't shake it. I curled up under the Afghan again and let thoughts of them two consume me until I drifted to sleep.

REMY

"Oooo shit! Ooo baby I missed this dick so much! Oh my God I can't take it. Please baby. I can't take no more dick daddy."

I rolled my eyes and kept fucking Dymond from the back slapping her ass in response. I wished she'd shut the fuck up with all this fake bs. She knew she was full of shit. She could take the dick just fine. I guess she thought she was stroking a nigga ego or something but I knew what the fuck I could do to her. She could take the dick and had been taking it for the last six months that I had been fucking with her ass. Every time I smashed, I left her ass damn near needing a wheel-chair and guess what? She would bring her ass right back for more so, I don't know where this whole she couldn't take the dick shit was coming from, but she could kill all that noise.

I had her bent over the bed with all of that ass in my face going to town on that pussy. I was grinding in that thing making it sound like somebody was mixing some macaroni and cheese; I was fucking her so good. The deeper that I dove in her pussy, the more that she screamed for more.

I swear I did not understand these hoes. One minute she screaming she can't take the dick, then she begging me not to stop. What is it with these crazy ass chicks?

I gave her the dick for a few more seconds, and when I knew I was about to bust, I pulled out and turned her ass around making her get on her knees. She opened her mouth wide ready for me to bust down her throat.

I snatched the condom off jacking my dick in my hand. She covered my dick with her mouth and sucked me so damn good I promise my toes was gripping the carpet. I bust down her throat letting her swallow a whole goddamn elementary school of kids. She gulped them all down smacking her lips and gave me a smile instantly bringing down my high..

Don't get me wrong, Dymond was gorgeous as a muthafucka. She was a baddie. I had been fucking with her ass for the past six months after meeting her at Onyx. Me and my boys had gone to the club the night before his wedding, and just about every nigga in the club was drooling off her. She was working the whole damn club and getting niggas to run they pockets.

She got all my partners, but she didn't get me. Fuck the bullshit. If you getting my money you fucking. Fuck that taking your clothes off shit. You take your clothes off then your payment is going to be some dick.

She tried everything to get me to get a dance from her, but I was chilling. Next thing I know, she sliding me her phone number before we leave. I hadn't really been fucking with any other females since I had lost my girlfriend a few years back. I would fuck with a bitch here and there just to get a nut, but it was never nothing serious. I wasn't trying to get into no relationship again.

A couple of nights later, I hit her up to see what she was talking about. After she got off work I rolled up on her at her crib and gave her the stroke. Since then that ass been hooked. I let it be known that I wasn't trying to wife her though. Who really going to wife a stripper? Not only that, but she was too out there. She liked getting attention from all these niggas. I could fuck that type of chick, but I couldn't fuck with her. I didn't want no broad that be flirting with a bunch of niggas. Even if that's how she got her money.

Still, I dicked her down, and she did everything I wanted. I would go chill with her every now and then at the club, but she still wasn't getting any coins from me. Nor would she. Hell no. I knew I wasn't the only one she was fucking with. Dymond's name was known in the streets of Charlotte.

When she finished draining me of my seeds, I walked into the bathroom to clean up. She was gasping for air and panting and doing all this extra shit while she sat down on the bed and I just closed the door so I could wash my dick. I had been sweating bullets and wearing her ass out for the last hour and a half. I was ready to go to sleep.

When I finished washing my dick, I opened the door to see that she had laid down on the bed and was dozing off.

"I hope her ass didn't think she was going to be spending the night." I mumbled walking to the living room.

I needed to find my phone so I could get her ass an Uber. She had taken one to get to the crib, and I guess she thought she was going to stay, but that shit was not about to happen. Not with this nigga here.

I grabbed my boxers from off the floor and slid them on, flopping down on the couch to grab my phone. I wanted to be by myself. I don't know why Dymond was always trying to stay over, but that shit was too much like a relationship for me. I was still trying to get over Nikki.

Me and Nikki had been together since our junior year of high school. She was the perfect girl. She made me laugh, smile, and I loved her more than anything. When she told me that she was pregnant our sophomore year in college, I was excited. We were both at Johnson C. Smith getting our degrees, and I promised her that she wouldn't have to worry about dropping out of school. I was going to be right there by her side while she was pregnant with my baby girl. And I was. Until she was eight months.

I was going to class to take an exam, and she had decided to run to the store to get some groceries. She never made it. Some drunk nigga ran a red light and hit her. They rushed her to the hospital, and she tried to fight for as long as she could. By the time I found out what was going on and got to the hospital, she and the baby had died.

It felt like everything in me was broken. I felt like a part of me died that day that I lost Nikki and my daughter. Since then, it's just been this emptiness. After that, I left school, and started hustling with my cousin. He was coming up in the drug game, and I just stopped giving a fuck. I didn't really tell my mama what I was into, but I think she knew. With the kind of lifestyle that I had, it came from selling bricks. Not working from 9 to 5. I knew my mom didn't like it, but at the end of the day, all she would say is that she would just pray that I got it together. It was just me. My folks were upset that I left school but, with everything that happened they understood. Losing Nikki was hard on them too because she was practically their daughter.

I wasn't no heavy big-time drug dealer, but I did enough so that I had my own shit and could help pay my parents bills. I'd even given my sister money for her to go to college. Ever since I left, they were cracking down on her ass to go to school. She chose to go out of state which was probably the smartest thing she could have done to avoid their constant fussing.

My mind went back to Nikki. Damn I miss her. I wished it was her that I was here with. Fucking with these chicks was cool and everything, but it was a temporary fix for me. I wanted my girl back. I wanted my family. Instead, some fuck nigga took that away in the blink of an eye. What made it so bad, was that the fool only got seven years. Apparently, that's what the justice system thought my girl and daughter's life was worth. A lousy ass seven years. The minute that that idiot got out though? He was going to get his. I was going to make sure of that. No apology in the world was going to bring them back.

I could feel my eyes getting watery and blinked away the few tears that managed to escape.

"Why you sitting in here by yourself?"

I turned to see Dymond standing at the entrance of the living room. She was wearing a t-shirt that she had gotten out of my drawer and for some reason it just irritated the shit out of me. Normally it wouldn't have bothered me seeing as her ass was hanging out underneath, and all I could see was them sexy ass honey legs of hers with her hard nipples poking out, that would make me want to drag her ass back into the bedroom, but not tonight. I just wanted her ass gone.

"Aye yo Uber gonna be here in about six minutes." I said looking down at my phone.

"My what?" She said sounding like she was caught off guard.

"I called you an Uber to take you back to the crib." I told her not even looking at her.

She sucked her teeth and stomped over to where I was sitting.

"Soooo you was just going to make me leave without even saying something?" She said. "I thought we were going to go for round two?"

"Nah a nigga tired." I told her. "I got some shit I got to handle in a little bit. Plus you was the one that was back there saying you couldn't take the dick remember?" I reminded her.

The look on her face made me almost burst out laughing. That's what her ass get for lying and being all extra. I knew she was full of shit.

She started hissing and mumbling shit under her breath but I didn't care. Long as she got her ass dressed and left I was cool.

She finished throwing on her clothes seconds before the Uber pulled up.

"So I guess I'll just talk to you later then," she said with an attitude.

"Yeah I'll hit you up." I told her.

"Uh huh," she grunted walking out the door and slamming it behind her.

I smirked at her attitude. I knew her ass was feeling me but popping all that shit about us being just fuck buddies. Her ass was trying to be more than just a fuck buddy and she knew it. I was going to have to cut her off because I wasn't about to be dealing with this emotional bullshit. I never understand that when it came to females. If a nigga tell you what it is that we want or don't want, why females can't take it and just trust that shit? Nah. These chicks want to think that cause we fucking them that they belong to us or we belong to them. I don't belong to nobody. And it was going to stay that way.

I got up and locked the door and went to go lay down in my bed. I had to get up in a couple of hours and make some runs. But for now, I just wanted Nikki to consume my thoughts. I couldn't have her on this Earth, but I could still have her in my dreams.

SKYY

"Tierra, girl we've been here all night. My feet hurt. I'm ready to go."

"Girl it's only one o'clock! You act like you don't know how to have fun no more," she screamed over the music.

"Oh I know how to have fun. But, my feet don't! Got me wearing these five-inch stilettos knowing I can barely walk in them!" I laughed.

We had been at Royale for the last three hours and I was ready to go. My feet were on fire and I was walking around the damn club looking like a pterodactyl. I had decided to go out since Malachi went over to his parents house for dinner and he had planned on being a little late. I really didn't feel like being bothered with them tonight so I told him I was going to go hang with Tierra. Of course he had something to say, but I was going whether he liked it or not.

I waited until he left to get dressed because I didn't feel like arguing with him about what I was wearing. I had on a cute little black romper that stopped mid-thigh, and some matching black heels. I was only five foot four so the heels made me extremely tall; damn near Tierra's height. I had pressed out my hair but I had sweated out my edges as hot as it was.

I could just imagine what Malachi would say if he saw me. He was going to start harping on how I was dressed like some prostitute or something. Hell, Tierra was the one in here literally showing her ass. She had on the same romper that I did only hers was green. She was much taller than me and that thing barely covered her ass. I wasn't hating though. She had the body for it. Both of us looked good.

I just hoped that Malachi's ass was asleep when I got home because I damn sure didn't want to hear his mouth. I told him I wasn't going to stay out too late but Tierra and I lost track of time being at the club. I needed to have some fun though. It had been a couple of weeks since I had those nightmares, so going out with Tierra was just what I needed. Besides, it wasn't like I was entertaining any other man or anything like that. It was just a night out with my bestie. I hadn't seen her in forever, and I wanted to just catch up. We came to the club to dance, drink and have a good old time. But I was getting sleepy.

"Tierra I really need to get back to the house." I fussed. "It's late, Malachi gotta get up in the morning, and I got some stuff that I gotta handle."

"Oh alright already!" She sighed finishing her drink.

I waited for her to put a glass down at the bar and we finally maneuvered our way through the thick club to get outside to the car. The cool air hitting my skin felt so good. It was in the middle of July, and it was pretty hot outside during the day. With it being so late, of course the temperature had dropped a little but, it was hotter than Satan's toenails inside that club especially with all them black folks in there. I needed that air to cool off.

We walked to the car and I was dying to take my heels off. I would never understand why some women choose to walk around in these things every day. The minute that I closed the car door, I practically threw them muthafuckas in the backseat. Tierra hopped in and started to drive, and we headed towards my house. I could tell that she was agitated but, I was ready to go. She didn't have to deal with Malachi's ass; I did. And I didn't feel like dealing with the drama.

"Look T, I really appreciate you taking me out tonight. If you really want to stay, you know I don't mind taking an Uber or something." I offered.

She looked at me and rolled her eyes.

"Ain't nobody mad at you. And you damn sure ain't about to be out here taking no damn Uber. I just don't like the fact that this nigga controls you so damn much. Like you're your own person," she huffed.

"I know." I nodded. "But, it's just something that you have to do when you're in a relationship. You gotta be respectful and considerate of the other person."

"Respectful? Yes. Obedient? No," she corrected. "Skyy that nigga has you on lock and key."

"No he doesn't Tierra. And you know it's not like that." I corrected her.

"That's what it seems like. But, if that's how you want to look at it cool," she shrugged.

"T it's really not that bad." I told her. "It's just I try not to push his buttons."

"Shit you need to push something to get his old ass to loosen up," she smirked. "Sis that nigga act like he in his fifties instead of in his twenties."

"I know." I laughed. "But not all the time. Besides, he was there for me when nobody else was."

"Yeah but that doesn't mean that you got to just lie down and let him walk all over you either," she reasoned. "If he really wanted to be there for you, then he wouldn't have so many restrictions on you."

"I guess."

I just left it alone because I knew arguing would be pointless. They didn't get along and they would always have this crazy ass opinion of each other. I just wanted to drop it and enjoy the breeze.

"Girl tonight was so much fun." I mentioned.

"Yaaaassss!" she squealed. "I met this dude name Dartanian. Girl! He talking about taking me out to eat and everything tomorrow."

"You gonna go?" I asked sketchy.

"Hell yeah!" She laughed turning on my street. "You must not have been looking at what I was seeing. That boy was fine, and got money? Best believe I'm about to jump all over that."

We pulled up to the house, and the porch light was off.

"I swear I need to get me a man so I can move into a house like one of these," she said.

We lived off of Rocky River Road and the majority of the houses were big. Malachi wouldn't have it any other way.

"Aight girl let me tiptoe on in this house." I told her. "I'll call you later."

"All right girly," she said watching me as I made it up the walkway and into the house.

I turned the porch light on and heard her pull off.

It was pitch black in the house, so I figured Malachi was in bed asleep. I tiptoed through the hallways and jumped out of my skin when the light in the living room came on behind me.

"You do know that it's almost two in the morning right?" He asked.

"Malachi I'm sorry." I apologized. "Tierra and I were having fun and I told her I was ready to go but—"

"But you couldn't get home any other way other than waiting on your little trifling friend?" He said interrupting me.

"Okay seriously, I'm not even trying to do this tonight." I told him turning my back to him.

"So when are you trying to do it?" He questioned standing up and walking over to me. "Huh? Because you're the one that's out late not me. I've been sitting here waiting. You told me that you were going out with her for a little bit, and that you'd be back. And what the hell is this that you wearing?" He said looking at me up and down.

"It's a romper." I told him.

"It looks like you're wearing some damn swimsuit or something," he grimaced. "That's what you wore to go out with your friend? I don't even know why I'm surprised."

I leaned back against the wall and looked at him completely disgusted.

"What the hell is that supposed to mean? I'm not out here showing off my body or no shit like that. So, watch yourself Mr. *I got pictures of my coworker in a bikini in my phone."* I warned.

"Are we doing this whole ghetto talk thing again?" He said. "You dress like a stripper so now you want to talk like one?"

"You know what?" I stopped myself before I really went off. "I'm not doing this tonight. I'm tired and I just want to get some sleep. So, I'm going to take a shower and go to bed and we can talk about this later."

"No we're going to finish talking about this now," he said following behind me. "I don't want you hanging out with that ghetto ass girl anymore. Clearly she is trying to ruin our relationship."

"Trying to ruin our relationship?" I asked in disbelief spinning around. "Do you hear yourself right now? Really? One, the only one ruining anything is YOU with that bitch from your job. THAT'S what's ruining this relationship."

"I am not sleeping with Zoey!" he snapped. "Are you really that insecure?"

"Excuse me?" I hissed turning to look at this idiot. "I'm insecure now? I'm insecure because you're over here texting and talking to this little ass white bitch? Don't try that shit with me Malachi. You not gone flip this shit on me. Uh uh."

"So that's why you dressing like that and staying out late with somebody that doesn't respect the fact that you're in a relationship?" he pressed.

"God you act like I'm out with her all the time!" I sighed. "I go out with Tierra every now and then. I go to lunch with her like once a week. Other than that, I'm always here at home making sure you're taken care of. I don't have any friends EXCEPT Tierra. No family. No nothing. I take care of you all day every day. That's it."

I stopped and crossed my arms over my chest looking at him with the same hateful look he was giving me.

"Have you ever come home and not had your dinner ready or had a dirty house? No. I'm always here making sure you're good. I don't work because you don't want me to work. Every time I ask you can I go to school, it's a problem. So, if I go out with Tierra every now and then now it's a problem? Now she's causing problems in our relation-ship? But you and Zoey on some late night creep shit is cool? You're unbelievable."

"I'm not holding you prisoner Skyy," he rolled his eyes. "Stop being so dramatic."

"Okay, so now I'm being dramatic?" I asked. I couldn't help but to laugh at this fool. "I'm being dramatic but yet you're the one standing here telling me that I'm dressed like a hoe and trying to criticize me for coming in late when you got a whole bitch!"

"I am not sleeping with Zoey!" he yelled walking towards me.

"Bullshit!" I argued. "The only reason your ass is so riled up is because it's your guilty conscience from the shit you doing."

"Skyy—" he started.

"Uh uh." I stopped him. "Even if you weren't cheating with her Malachi, which I find that extremely hard to believe, you're still too overbearing and controlling. You still talk to me like I'm one of your employees."

"Because it's two in the damn morning!" He snapped. "Anything could have happened to you. I don't know where you are or if you're okay. You're out with your little friend who clearly doesn't care about the fact that you have a loving man at home who wants to make sure you are good."

"Malachi please! You didn't want to make sure that I was okay." I argued. "If you were really worried you would have called my phone, but you didn't. Instead you sat here in the dark waiting for me to come home so that you could start yelling at me like I was some child or something. Newsflash? I'm not your kid. But the way you act and scold me, I might as well be. You act like I'm supposed to have a curfew or something. You act like I'm just supposed to do whatever you say."

"Alright, you need to watch who you're talking to," he inter-rupted. "I don't know what's gotten into you lately, but all I'm asking is that you be considerate. All I'm saying is that I don't want you to be caught up with your friends to where you forget that you have a man at home. A man that provides for you by the way. A man that takes care of you. A man that gives you everything you want."

"Everything I want except freedom!" I yelled. "I can't do half of what I want to do for fear of your degrading remarks or you putting me down. I'm sick of it Malachi! Do I love you? Yes. But not to be dealing with this for the rest of my life. I'm not even 25 years old and I swear I feel like I'm 55. I do everything that you ask of me with no question. But once It's my turn to ask for something, it's a big fucking deal." I ranted.

I was going so fast it was like I was out of breath. But I had some shit to get off my chest.

"I put up with a lot from you because you're always reminding me of how you take care of me." I said. "What? Did you save me that day just so you could make me your personal little maid? Pick the poor little ghetto girl in the projects up from off of the streets, clean her up and then make her a modern-day slave?"

He looked at me and didn't say anything.

"What's the matter? Cat got your tongue now?" I asked, my arms still folded across my chest.

I don't know what came over me, but everything was just coming out.

"I swear to God I hate it here. I hate the way you treat me." I hissed. "I hate the way you control me."

He slowly nodded his head and walked past me as I continued to go off. Once he entered the bedroom and opened the closet that had all of my belongings in it, he removed two suitcases from the top shelf and tossed them onto the bed.

"What are you doing?" I asked him.

He ignored me and started yanking all of the clothes that were hanging in the closet down and throwing them into the suitcases.

"What the hell are you doing?" I yelled this time.

He continued to ignore me which only pissed me off more. Once I realized what was actually going on I totally lost it.

"Oh so you packing my shit now?" I snapped. "Really Malachi? Really nigga? You just going to sit here and put me out? You low down dirty mutha...You know what? I'm not even about to go there. It's cool. Since you want me out so bad...allow me to help."

With tears now streaming from my eyes, I grabbed an armful of my clothes and started to throw them into the luggage as well.

After both of the suitcases were stuffed with my things, Malachi zipped them up, carried them to the front door and tossed them outside. I stormed past him to grab them off of the lawn and he stood staring at me with this pained look in his eyes.

"I love you Skyy," he said slowly. "But, I'm not about to keep someone here who doesn't want to be here. It's pretty obvious that loving me and being in a relationship with me is something that you don't want. So since you're not happy here, you don't have to be here."

I was trying not to break down because I knew I did say everything that he just repeated.

"So this is what you do?" I asked straining to keep my composure."Put me out without trying to find some sort of resolution?"

"It's not what *I* did Skyy...It's what *you* chose."

He closed the door and left me standing there with my entire life in two bags.

REMY

"Sooo you gonna come over later and see me?"

"Ion know man. I might. I gotta handle some shit real quick but I should be able to." I told her.

"Well I hope so. You know it's been a couple of weeks since I had that dick," she mentioned.

"That's cause your ass been tripping." I grumbled.

"I'm sorry baby," she apologized. "You know I just be doing too much sometimes."

"Yeah. All the time." I added.

I was talking to Dymond on the phone after leaving the club. She had been hitting me up since the last time I saw her, trying to apologize and everything. Her ass was getting way too clingy and I needed to cut her loose. I wasn't trying to deal with no Fatal Attraction type broad and that's exactly what she was turning into.

Every time I came to the club, she was cutting eyes at me and acting all mushy and shit. God forbid another bitch be up in my face she was ready to spit fire.

She was talking aimlessly on the phone and I was just sitting there listening as I drove. It was almost four in the morning, and I knew she would be getting off soon so I was gonna drop by her crib and get my dick wet real quick. I just hoped she wasn't on no other shit.

When I first started fucking around with her everything was good. Now she was acting like I was her nigga or something. She could let one of these corny ass dudes from the club be her nigga cause I wasn't with it.

"I can't wait to see you baby. I hope you do come cause damn I miss tasting that dick," she cooed. "I gotta show you how sorry I am. Ooo baby I can't wait to get my lips around that big thick dick."

"Oh word?" I said turning back to the conversation.

I was driving down Harris Blvd right before it connected to Plaza Road, and I almost didn't notice ole girl until I saw a group of niggas about twenty feet behind her. It was some light-skinned chick with suitcases walking down the street. She looked like she had been crying from what I could see. It was dark and I wasn't up on her, but I could tell she was obviously upset about something.

Damn. I wondered why she was out here so late.

I was more so concerned about the niggas behind her. It was three little wiry niggas all dressed in dark clothing following at a distance behind her. It didn't take a genius to figure out that they were about to rob her ass. I mean she looked like an easy target. She wasn't paying attention to anything around her, and she was drawing hella attention to herself with two big ass Louis Vuitton bags. I didn't know old girl, but I damn sure didn't want to see anything happen to her.

I forgot that Dymond was still on the phone talking about all the shit that she wanted to do until I heard my name being called. I guess I had tuned her out when I noticed this girl.

"Remy? Baby? Did you hear me?"

"Yeah." I said quickly.

"No you didn't. You didn't hear nothing I said," she argued.

"I said I heard you!" I snapped. "Look I'll be over there in a little bit. Let me call you back I got to handle some shit real quick."

I hung up the phone before she could say anything else and pulled up on the girl. I parked my car right there in the middle of the street throwing on my hazards and hopped out. She jumped seeing me, and stood frozen.

"Aye yo, I'm not trying to scare you or nothing like that, but you got three niggas behind you right now a good little ways back that probaly been following you for a minute." I told her. "I don't know if you looking to get jacked, but that's exactly what's going to happen if you keep walking up the street like this."

She looked around nervous and I could tell now that I had a closer look she had been crying. Her eyes were puffy, and she looked exhausted.

"I wasn't even paying attention," she said barely above a whisper. "I was just trying to get in touch with my friend to see if she could pick me up."

"Well, I don't know where your friend at but, I don't think it's too smart for you to be out here by yourself." I told her.

I looked back to see the niggas watching me. I had my pistol so I wasn't worried about shit if they tried to run up.

"You ain't got nobody else you can call or anything?" I asked.

"No, only my best friend but she's not answering the phone," she replied. "Me and my boyfriend just got into a fight, and he put me out."

"Damn, that's fucked up." I mumbled.

This was some real fuck nigga shit. Then again, I didn't know their situation. Hell she could have got this nigga for his paper or fucked one of his boys or something, I don't know. Looking at her though, she didn't really strike me as the type. She seemed kind of naive and sheltered.

"Well, look I ain't tryna get in your business or nothing but you about to be hitting Milton Road and being out here, all it's going to get you is robbed or worse." I advised.

She looked down at herself and groaned in frustration.

"I didn't plan on getting into an argument with him," she sniffed. "And I damn sure didn't plan on being out here. I probably look like some hooker or something."

I couldn't help but to smirk at her speech. She sounded so proper. Now I knew she wasn't the average chick.

"Well, I know you don't know me or anything, but if you need it, I can give you a ride to your friend's house." I offered.

She looked at me skeptical and I saw fear for the first time.

"It's late and... I don't know if I should," she hesitated.

"Well, normally you shouldn't. But, if you want to take your chances with them niggas lurking back there, I can almost guarantee that if I pull off, they coming for you." I warned.

She started fidgeting and looking like she was completely lost. I wasn't about to force her to get in the car. I was just trying to help her out. If she wanted to get robbed by them niggas, then that was on her.

"Are you sure it won't be a problem?" She asked after a few seconds.

"Nah. You good." I told her. "I was going to the crib anyway so I'll just consider this my good deed of the day."

I grinned at her and she gave me a small smile.

"Well, I'd really appreciate it," she said. "My feet are KILLING me and I am not trying to be out here looking like some streetwalker."

I nodded my head and reached over to take her bags.

"I feel you."

"Do you need gas money or anything?" She offered.

"Oh nah you good." I told her walking over and opening the door for her to get in.

My phone was vibrating in my pocket, and I already knew that it was Dymond's ass calling me back. I watched the girl get into the car and couldn't help but to admire her frame. Even though she was all puffy-eyed, she was real pretty. Like that angelic kind of pretty. She was a little on the short side and had a real petite frame. Her hair looked real, and I didn't really see a lot of makeup on her. She looked kind of young.

I closed the door and walked around to the driver's side.

Whoever this girl's boyfriend was, he was on some next level shit. I don't know why I cared knowing that I shouldn't, but I did. She was too innocent to be out there like that.

I looked at her out of the corner of my eye as she gave me her friend's address.

Damn. The more I looked at her the more I wondered how old she was? She looked like she was barely legal.

A lot of these girls was out here looking a lot older than what they actually were, and a nigga wasn't trying to be on no R.Kelly shit.

Dymond called my phone again, and I ignored it. I would get up with her another time. I just hoped that my black ass wasn't about to help this girl out and end up in jail my damn self.

SKYY

"You okay over there?" I heard.

"Not really." I admitted. "I'm just kind of blown with all of this."

I was sitting in the front seat of some strangers Suburban and didn't even know his name. I couldn't believe that Malachi put me out like that. The one time I stood up for myself, he acted like I said something so wrong.

Who puts their girlfriend out at two in the morning?

When he closed the door in my face I was in so much shock that I just started walking and wasn't even paying attention to where I was going. I didn't really have anybody that I could call. I had been calling Tierra's phone non-stop with no success. I was hoping she would answer her door especially since he was driving me there. If she didn't, I didn't know what I was going to do. I wasn't about to go to Malachi's parents' house because of course they would take his side. And I damn sure wasn't about to go crawling back to him. If that's how he felt and if he wanted to be that way, then to hell with him. I had my clothes and about $100 in cash on me. I just hope to God that he didn't take my name off of the accounts.

I should go to the ATM and get out all the cash that I can just to piss him off.

I couldn't believe his ass didn't even care that I was out here in the streets this late at night. Thank God this man came along to give me a ride. What if I was walking and those guys robbed me or tried to rape me? It would have been his fault if something had happened to me. He probably didn't care that some stranger was even giving me a ride.

"I'm sorry. I just got in the car with you and didn't even ask your name." I told the stranger.

"Remy," he said looking over at me.

"Like the liquor?" I asked.

He smirked and nodded his head focusing on the road.

"Yeah," he smiled as the GPS led him to my best friend's house.

"Oh wow okay." I giggled. "So, what's your last name? VSOP?"

He looked at me out the corner of his eye, and I stopped laughing.

"I'm sorry." I said offering an apology. "I know that was a corny joke."

"Very," he nodded. "But it's cool. My last name is Deveaux."

"Got you." I paused. "Well I'm Skyy. Skyy Pearson."

He snorted and I looked at him confused.

"What was that about?" I asked.

"Yo, how you gonna clown me when you named after a liquor your damn self?" he laughed. "You white liquor and I'm dark."

I smiled a little at the irony.

"Touche'." I agreed.

We rode in silence as the GPS continued to direct him and I just stared out the window.

"So uh, what was you and your man fighting about?" he pried. "Did he cheat on you or something?"

"I don't even know." I admitted. "He said he didn't, but it was that and...a whole lot of other bullshit."

He looked at me funny like he wanted to pry some more but, I ignored him and turned my attention back to the window.

"We should be pulling up to her house in a minute." I told him.

"Thank you again for your help tonight. If you didn't show up, I don't know what would have happened."

"Well for one you and your Louis bags probably would have been snatched," he pointed out. "You gotta be careful. I don't know your situation with your dude or nothing but, any nigga that put his girl out on the streets or lets his girl out on the streets for whatever this late at night, that ain't no man to me. Especially one that looks like you."

I whipped my head in his direction wondering where he was going with his little statement.

"And what is that supposed to mean?" I asked.

"No disrespect or nothing like that yo," he said. "I meant that you are a very pretty woman. It's late and you're dressed up, so I'm just assuming you went to a party or something. And not everybody in Charlotte going to have a good guy vibe, you just happen to meet one in me" he went on with a smile. "It's some folks out there that will try to get at you. Especially when you walk around with $5,000 luggage, you feel me?"

He really had a point. I guess I had jumped to the extreme.

"Well, like I said it was just a disagreement." I reiterated. "I'm sure he'll probably call me tomorrow to apologize. We'll work it out."

"I guess," he shrugged his shoulders. "That ain't none of my business."

We rode the last few minutes in silence, and I glanced at him. He was an okay looking dude. He looked like he lived at the gym. He had a whole bunch of tattoos! It was damn near covering all of his skin. There was one huge tat on his left arm that had a girl named Nikki on it. I'm sure it was his baby mama. He looked like he had a few of those. Shoot, he looked like the type of dude that would rob somebody. Silently I was praying that it wouldn't be me.

"You got a lot of tattoos." I observed.

"Yeah," he laughed. "They can get addictive."

"They look painful." I said frowning.

"Pain is relative," he reasoned. "What man can't deal with a tattoo?"

"You sure do have a lot of definitions on what a man is and isn't." I pointed out.

"Just how I am," he answered.

"That's her house right there." I said pointing to the small brick house on the corner.

I was happy to see her Maxima parked. He pulled up into the driveway, and I got out praying to God that she would answer the door. I had texted her a few times to let her know that I was on the way and she still hadn't answered. I really hope that she would wake up because I had no place else to go.

I got ready to grab my bags, and he offered his assistance.

"Thanks again for the ride. Are you sure I can't give you gas money or anything?" I asked.

"I told you I'm good," he argued. "You want me to hang around and wait to make sure you make it in?" He said motioning towards the door.

"No I should be fine." I assured him. "I'm sure you got to get back to whatever you were doing."

I wanted to mention his phone going off non-stop in the truck but that wasn't my business.

"Aight then," he said placing my luggage down next to me. "Well be careful. Hope you and your dude work things out."

"Thanks." I said giving him a smile.

I walked towards the door dragging my suitcases and could feel him watching me. I knocked and stood praying that she would answer. This was so embarrassing. I could feel his eyes on me.

I knocked a few more times and took several deep breaths. I didn't want to turn around and tell him that she wasn't home.

Why couldn't he have just pulled off? I told him I was straight!

"Everything good?" He called out.

I sighed and tapped my foot on the ground for a few seconds.

God what am I going to do?

I turned around to see him standing watching me.

"So, she's not answering her door." I said as I walked back in his direction.

He looked like he was agitated but he didn't say anything. He was standing looking like one of those models off Instagram with the whole semi-baggy sweats and fitted shirt look.

"Look, I'm sorry about all of this." I sighed. "I know this is really taking up a lot of your time. I can catch a cab or an Uber or something. Or I'll just wait here until she wakes up."

"You going to wait outside all night until you home girl wakes up?" He asked looking at me skeptical.

"Well I just don't want to take up any more of your time." I told him pushing my hair out of my face.

"So do you have anywhere else to go?" He asked.

"Not really." I admitted shaking my head. "Honestly, I don't have any family here, and outside of my boyfriend, my best friend is pretty much the only person that I talk to. I don't really know a lot of people."

I didn't know if I was giving him too much information but, I just knew that I was tired. I wanted to lay down and go to sleep. The question was, where?

"Umm I hate to be a bother but, do you think that maybe you could take me to a hotel close by?" I pressed. "That way I can just get a room or something until tomorrow."

"Yeah that's cool," he agreed. "It's a couple of hotels up a few blocks by the University area."

"Great." I got back in the car and once again he threw my bags in the back seat of the truck. "I feel so bad. I know I am really messing up your night."

His phone buzzed again and he looked at the caller ID frowning.

"I'm assuming that's probably your girlfriend the way it's been ringing?" I asked.

"Nah hell nah," he shook his head quickly. "I don't do the girlfriend thing."

He looked like the player type so I wasn't surprised.

I sent Tierra a text message letting her know to call me when she woke up and thought about my argument with Malachi as we drove. He was busy texting and driving so I wasn't the focus of attention.

Was I overreacting? I don't think that what I said was wrong. How could he just trip like that?

He had to understand that he was being controlling. He had to understand that I was tired of being under his thumb. It wasn't that I didn't love him, I was just tired of being treated like a child.

Remy took me to the Drubury behind the TGIF restaurant and followed me inside to the front desk so that I could get a room. I pulled out my debit card to pay and yawned in anticipation thinking about the hot shower that I was ready to take. The clerk was looking at me and Remy with a curious expression. It was late and I did look a mess. She probably thought I was some low budget hoe or something.

"I'm sorry ma'am but this card has been declined," she said interrupting my thoughts.

"What?" I said looking at her confused.

"Yes ma'am it's showing declined," she repeated.

"Can you run it again?"

"Okay."

She rolled her eyes with an attitude but did as I asked. A few seconds later she shook her head handing me the card back.

"Sorry. Still declined."

I was turning red from embarrassment and frustration.

Remy was a few feet away talking on the phone, and I was praying that he hadn't heard anything that she said. He looked like he was having an in-depth conversation with someone he really didn't want to have one with. Right when I turned to look at him of course he looked up at me.

"Let me call you back," he said to whoever was on the phone. He hung up and walked over looking between me and the clerk. "What's the problem?"

"My card was declined." I mumbled. "But it's okay I got cash."

"I'm sorry," the clerk interrupted. "We can't take cash. Cash is only accepted for deposits."

"How much is the room?" He yawned.

"Remy no! I can't let you do that." I refused.

39

"Well what else you gonna do?" he questioned. "Cause you don't have much choice at this point."

"I can pay for it." I insisted. "I just don't know what's going on with the card. I probably just got to call customer service or something."

He pulled me away from the desk and looked down at me.

"Didn't you say that you and your man got into a fight?" He asked.

"Yeah." I said looking embarrassed.

The hotel clerk was eavesdropping trying to listen to our conversation.

"I'm assuming your name was on his shit?" he pressed.

"Yes." I sighed rubbing my head in frustration.

Shit. This Negro took my name off of the account. He was really showing his ass right now.

"I cannot believe that he did this shit." I hissed.

He walked over to the clerk and she eagerly straightened up.

"How much is one of the rooms?" He asked.

"We've got a double bedroom for $94 plus tax," she told him looking at her computer screen.

She was batting her eyes and flirting but clearly, he wasn't picking up on it.

He took his wallet out handing her the card for her to charge.

"Are you sure?" I asked him. "You've already helped me enough."

"Yo trust I'm good. If I wasn't I wouldn't have offered," he told me. "At least this way I know you good so when I roll out I ain't gotta worry about seeing you on the news or no shit like that."

"Thank you so much." I said. "I promise I will pay you back. Tomorrow I'm going to get this all straightened out."

"Don't worry about it," he dismissed. "It ain't no big thing."

"Well it is to me." I said sincerely. "Thank you."

The clerk handed me the key card and I sniffed holding back the tears I was trying not to cry. I was so furious with Malachi's ass. Not only was he okay with putting me out, but he took my name off the cards?

At least I had somewhere to lay my head for the night. I would call

Tierra tomorrow and ask her if I could stay with her for a while until I could figure out what I was going to do.

He followed me to the elevator and helped me get my stuff in the room. Both of us were yawning at this point. It was almost five in the morning.

"Thank you again." I urged. "I really appreciate it."

"Here put my number in your phone," he demanded taking my phone out of my hand and programming it. "Give me a holler in the morning if you need anything."

"Trust me, you've done more than enough." I said. "I'm going to be okay. I'm sure once my bestie wakes up in the morning she'll see the thousand missed calls and come get me."

"All right," he nodded. "Well, I'll let you go ahead and get your sleep."

"Thanks."

I walked him to the door and locked it behind him. I was ready to pass out!

I flopped down on the bed and sent Malachi a text message going off on him for taking me off of the accounts. He had shown me what I really meant to him, so as far as I was concerned, I was done. I had no idea where I was going, but I knew he wasn't it.

I hopped in the shower and changed into some comfortable clothes to sleep in. Before my head hit the pillow, I was out like a light.

REMY

"I've been calling your ass all night. How come you wasn't answering your damn phone? And why did you just hang up on me earlier? You told me that you were coming over here. I done got off work and was sitting at the damn house waiting on you, and you weren't even answering your phone! Like what's really good?"

"Is your ass gone be quiet long enough for me to talk?" I asked.

I was on my way to the crib when Dymond called me for the sixth time. She was all rowdy but shit, it's not like I ever said that I was for sure going over there.

"I mean I'm saying Remy. You done had me waiting all night on you. Shit I could have stayed at the club and made some extra money or something. Or I could have went with my homegirl to this private party that she was doing," she complained.

"Didn't nobody tell you to wait for me." I told her. "See that's the shit right there I'm talking about. You don't listen. I never said that I was coming. I told you I was thinking about it and that I had some shit that I had to handle."

She sucked her teeth and got quiet. Finally.

"Yo I'm tired." I said trying to be nice. "I'ma just holla at you later."

I meant later like never.

"So you not coming through?" she asked.

"Didn't I just say—no. I'm not. I'm too tired."

This broad was like hard of hearing or some shit.

"Whatever," she mumbled.

"Look, I'm bout to go to the crib and catch some sleep. I had a long night."

"What were you doing that was just so important that you couldn't make it over here?" She asked.

"Minding my fucking business." I told her. "Yo, what's with this questioning me shit?"

"Baby I wasn't questioning you damn!" she screeched. "I just meant maybe you could have come by that's all. Even if it's just for a couple of minutes."

"I just told you that I couldn't." I groaned.

Why in the fuck was I arguing with this girl? Shit, how many times could I say I wasn't pulling up on her ass?

I drove down 85 so I could head to the crib and rushed to get her off of my phone.

"I'm about to go to bed. I ain't got time for this arguing shit." I told her. "I'ma just chill on you for a minute cause right now you being real extra."

"How am I extra?" She asked. "All I asked was for you to come through. You act like I'm asking you to walk down the aisle or something."

"Yo, I'ma be real with you Dymond. You cool and everything. But I told you, I don't answer to nobody." I reminded her. "I'm not looking for no girlfriend or no relationship. None of that shit. So if we fucking, cool. That's what it is. But all this clingy shit...you doing too much. Like all that whining and shit because I'm not up under you all the time? Niggas in relationships do that shit. Not me. You knew what it was. And let's be real, you got other niggas on the side anyway."

"Oh my God Remy," she dragged. "Nobody said anything about a relationship. I'm just saying that you know I'm feeling you. But, if you ain't feeling me like that, then it can be just sex."

I rolled my eyes because I knew she was full of shit. There was no way in the world that this bitch could just get some dick and not be attached. She had already put the shit out there. Yeah, I was going to have to fall back from her ass. Like a nigga was going to have to change phone numbers and all kinds of shit. I had fucked up letting her come to the crib. That was the green light for her. She knew where a nigga lived.

"Yo, I'ma holla at you later. It's late as shit and I need to get some sleep because I got a lot of shit to handle tomorrow."

"Okay," she replied sounding disappointed.

I hung up and made the drive to the crib. A nigga was tired. It would have been nice to slide up in some pussy, but after driving all over Charlotte to help a girl I didn't even know, I was about to shut it down.

I didn't realize it but, I wondered about her. She seemed real sweet and innocent. She was real proper too. Even listening to her curse was funny. She was like a reality Disney character or something. She wasn't like most of these females that I had met or seen. I could tell that she was embarrassed and really hurt by the shit that her nigga did.

When she told me about her and her man getting into it and having a disagreement, that's when I knew that she was different. Females that I met didn't say shit like "disagreements". Them hoes was beefing with they niggas.

Yeah she was cute. She had to be mixed with something because she had these little freckles that I noticed on her nose. I laughed at the fact that she made fun of my name but was named after a liquor her damn self.

She kind of reminded me of Nikki with the way she seems so reserved and always seeing the bright side to shit. Nikki was very optimistic about things. She always saw the good in people. Her mother felt like I should forgive the fool that took her and my baby from me because she would want to forgive them. That's one thing I couldn't do though.

I pulled up to my complex and parked dragging myself out the truck. Even though I was hustling and making good money, I didn't like to draw attention to myself. I had a regular ass apartment and lived as basic as possible. Eventually I would probably want to get a house and all that, but for what? Right now it was just me. And I didn't see myself settling down any time soon so I was cool on that.

I walked into the apartment and headed straight for the shower. I needed that hot water to hit my skin and relax me so that I could get some sleep. I had to hit the streets tomorrow.

By the time I was done it was a quarter to five. I had promised my mother that I was going to go to some special service that she was having at her church, and she was not about to let me out of it. I had to be at her crib at nine in the morning. If I even thought about telling her that I wasn't going to make it, she would come snatch me out of my bed and whoop my ass. My mama was the only woman that could still put me in check. Call me a mama's boy, but I was going to be there.

I laid down enjoying the comfort of the sheets in my king size bed, and my thoughts went back to Skyy. I hoped she was good. I felt kind of bad for her when she said she didn't have anybody. She looked too young to be out here by herself. She looked like she was barely out of her teens. With the way these chicks out here was getting snatched up and put into human trafficking, I hoped she paid more attention and looked out for herself.

A girl like her could not handle the streets.

SKYY

"Skyy, how long do you plan on ignoring me? I've called you every day for the past week at least four or five times a day and you haven't returned any of my calls. I know that things got a little heated, but the least you could do is call me back and let me know you're okay. I know you're probably at your... friend's house but, would you please just call me back? I know it's probably hard for you right now but, I still love you and I think we should just talk about this. So, call me back."

I rolled my eyes at the voicemail that Malachi had left me. It had been a week since I had left his house, and he had been calling me every day all day, that much was true. Every single voicemail he was telling me how I needed to come home and that I overreacted. I didn't overreact. He was the one who put my ass out. What I look like going back to him after everything that he did?

He disrespects me, belittles me, packs my shit and puts it out of the house, then cuts off my access to all of the bank accounts. If it wasn't for Tierra my phone would be off. Thank God I had enough sense to get the phone turned on in my name otherwise that would probably be gone too. I don't know what was going on in his head.

I deleted the message and hung up the phone, not wanting to deal with his bullshit.

"Let me guess." Tierra said looking at me from her chair. "Another message from Mr. Bipolar?"

"Yeah." I grunted. "He's talking about how I need to call him back and that we need to talk and that I overreacted and all of that. But I didn't overreact. Oh, and he knows that I'm over here." I added.

"Girl fuck him!" She stressed. "I know he better not bring his square-headed Carlton Banks looking ass over here. I ain't scared of his ass."

"T, I'm not saying I'm scared of him." I huffed.

"Oh, I know you not," she agreed. "But as far as I'm concerned, his ass needs to stay over there where he belongs. He fucked up. And he knows he fucked up that's why he's calling you every damn day all hours of the night." She started flipping through the channels with the remote. "Nah fuck that. His ass needs to suffer."

"I just don't understand how he can really think that he can just control me like that." I stressed. "After three years, he just does not get it. Aside from you I don't have anybody. I can't even get a job because every single application that I put in, I'm being rejected. All I have is a GED. And the only experience I have work wise, is for his dad's company. So, even if I tried to get a job somewhere else, they wouldn't hire me."

"They might," she reasoned fixing her nails.

"Girl do you know how many job applications I put in this week?" I told her.

"Well where have you been looking?" she asked.

"I've looked everywhere. Law firms, hospitals, hell even McDonalds." I sighed. "Imagine me coming home smelling like greasy burgers every day? I'd never be able to afford my own place."

"Girl why are you in such a hurry to get your own place?" She asked. "You know you can stay here. It's plenty of room. You ain't gotta worry about being up under Malachi all hours of the day. You can come and go as you please."

"Yeah but, I don't want to be depending on you."

"Skyy, come on we're girls. You know I got you," she said coming over to sit next to me. "I'm just glad that you ain't got to keep dealing with his stuck-up snobby ass. Yo, he looks like he walks around with a stick in his ass."

"I swear I can't stand you." I burst out laughing.

I was glad to have a friend like Tierra. She had been by my side since that morning. The night I came to her house, her car was there but, she had hooked up with the guy she met at the club and gone to his spot. As soon as she turned her phone on and found out that I was at the hotel, she came and got me. I had been staying with her ever since.

Every day I was sitting in the house watching TV, filling out applications online on her laptop and every day Malachi was calling me and I was curving his ass. At first, I thought about going back to him, but I knew that things weren't going to change. He would still be lying to me. He would still be disrespecting me. He would still be cheating. I needed to do for myself. I wanted to be independent like my friend.

She was a beautician and could hook up some hair. She was also going to school online. I didn't have anything. But, that was going to change.

"So, what do you want to do?" She asked bringing me out my trance.

"I don't know." I admitted. "I really want to get a job, but I don't know what I could do. I mean like I said the only thing I'm qualified to do is working at a fast-food joint. And I know you said I could stay here and everything but eventually I do want to get my own place. I'm tired of depending on people T. I don't want to keep going to other people for help. I want to be able to do for myself and not have to worry about asking somebody for money or wondering if somebody's going to cut something off."

"I feel you," she nodded slowly. "I mean, I can understand what you're saying. Like I said you know I'm always going to have your back and anything you need I got you. Don't worry it's not going to be like this forever."

"I hope not." I said. "Cause I'm going to make damn sure that I don't go through this again and I refuse to go crawling back to his ass."

"Good," she sternly said agreeing with me.

"Now I just need to figure out how I can make some quick cash." I announced.

"Well…" she said hesitantly.

"Well what?" I asked side eyeing her.

"I mean, I know a couple of spots that could use some cute girls," she answered.

"Umm cute girls for what?" I said looking at her confused.

"Well…you got a cute face and a banging ass body. And, you know, I know a couple of people that work up at Onyx. They could use some new faces. You'd make a killing," she tried to insist.

"Wait." I said trying to hold in my laugh. "You talking about going to work at a strip club?"

"Yeah," she nodded. "Why not? It's the easy way to make quick cash. All you gotta do is go in there and toot that thing up one good time. Girl you cute! It'll be easy for you to make some money," she squealed.

"Okay, so let's talk about how there are several things wrong with that suggestion." I started.

"Like what?" She asked getting up to go to the kitchen.

"Well for one, have you forgotten that I dance like a white girl?" I laughed.

She burst out laughing as she headed to the refrigerator.

"Yeah I did forget about that. But you know I can teach you some stuff," she insisted. "Trust me, niggas ain't really worried about you dancing anyway. All they want to do is see you get naked and throw bills. And with all that ass you dragging? You could get your rent paid for the whole year in like a week."

"I barely take my clothes off for Malachi's ass. What makes you think I'm going to want to do it in front of strangers? I don't want them touching me and stuff." I fussed.

"You know you watch too many BET movies," she laughed. "It ain't nothing like that. You going to be up on a stage, and they're going to be throwing money at you. I'm telling you. You can make some money."

"Um yea sis, thanks but no thanks."

She grabbed a couple of sodas from the fridge and headed back to the living room. There was no way that I would ever think about doing something like that. I could only imagine Malachi's reaction. He would probably have a heart attack. Then again, why the hell am I still worried about what he's going to think? He was no longer a factor.

"All I'm saying is, just try it for maybe a week," she said handing me one of the drinks and flopping down on the couch. "I got a homegirl that work up there. Well she used to. She cute just like you and got a body just like yours. That girl was making damn near two grand a night."

"What?" I choked on a mouthful of soda.

I ain't going to front. The thought of making that much money in a night was kind of appealing. But, I was still very much hesitant.

"I don't know Tierra." I told her. "I know how you and your friends are. And I would be so damn nervous." I responded as my phone began to vibrate once again. I reached down to see another text for Malachi.

Chi: " *Look I ain't going to keep calling your lil ass, I know you don't have any money and that broke bitch you call a friend ain't going to be able to keep your weak ass up for long. So do yourself and her a favor and come on home while I'm still letting you.*"

I wouldn't say it was a sign from God, but it was a sign that it was time for me to grow up. I couldn't believe that he had called me weak. But then again I never gave him any reason to think that I was strong. I was fed up with feeling like I was anyone's charity case. It was time for Skyy Pearson to grow the fuck up and become the woman that I knew I could be.

"So tell me how this works," I asked with more confidence in my voice.

"Girl, all you gotta do is get you a couple of drinks in you, and just relax," she advised. "Act like you dancing at home in front of a mirror or something. And you know I can teach you how to twerk. Honey by the time I'm done with you, you're gonna be the next Cardi B."

"Girl, if you turn me into Cardi B, I'ma call your ass Houdini bitch because that's going to be some pure magic."

We both laughed, and she turned on some music.

"Come on, I'm going to teach you how to twerk."

I was nervous as all get out as we spent the next couple of hours dancing and laughing. She actually taught me how to twerk. It wasn't as complicated as I thought it would be.

I don't know if it was Malachi's text or the fact that for the first time in my life I wanted to be able to fully take care of myself, but I was going to try to work at the strip club.

If I can make two grand in a night, what could I possibly lose?

REMY

GIVE ME A LITTLE SOMETHING TO REMEMBER (CARDI!)

Tryna make love in a Sprinter (yeah)
Quick to drop a nigga like Kemba (go)
Lookin' like a right swipe on Tinder (woo)
Shit on these hoes (shit)
Light up my wrist on these hoes (wrist)
Now I look down on these bitches (down)
I feel like I'm on stilts on these hoes (woo)

"Aye yo, let me get a double of Hennessy on the rocks." I told the waitress trying to talk over the music.

"Aight I got you. Anything else?" She asked bending down and putting her titties in my face.

"Yeah let me get your number with your fine ass!" My boy Dante yelled.

Everybody sitting by us started laughing and she rolled her eyes. These niggas was twisted. Me, Dante and my cousin Dre had come to Onyx about an hour before to kick it and hustle a little bit. Supposedly there was a nigga named Tommy going around the club claiming to have better product than me and I wanted to check things out while my boys got bent.

Dante was grabbing for the agitated waitress drunk as shit.

"I'll be back with your drinks in a minute," she said with an attitude snatching away.

I shook my head at these two drunk fools and leaned back in my seat. They had been hanging around all day and were getting on my nerves. Dre was dodging his baby mama so they came intruding on me at my folks house and of course my mama being who she was wanted to feed everybody. My mama would not go more than a few days without fussing at me to come see her. Though my father was there and she was healthy as a horse, she would always pull her "getting older" card on me.

Even though I was out here hustling, I always made sure to see my folks at least once a week and my mama would guilt me into going to church with her at least once a month. Every now and then I would check on Nikki's mom Kim. Though Nikki was gone, I still loved Kim. She was like a second mother to me. She had left Charlotte after Nikki died and moved back to Atlanta. Whenever I would make a run to the A, I would swing through and make sure she was good.

I did all of this but to the outside world, I was just that hustling ass nigga that didn't give a fuck about nobody. I didn't allow anybody to get close because that's how you get fucked up; especially in this business. I liked my life just like it was. I did my shit, I stayed low key, I got pussy here and there, and I got my money.

"Yo I gotta make a run to Boston next week. You rolling with me?" Dre asked me.

"Yea I got you." I told him taking a puff of my cigar.

I watched the dancers walking past showing off new asses and titties. I was trying to go hustle but, Dre avoiding his baby mama needed an excuse and well, he was my cousin so here we were. I was ready to go because as usual, Dymond had been on her bullshit and all up under a nigga. The minute she found me walking in, she was all giggly and shit. I still wasn't trying to fuck with her though. I just wanted to hang out at the club, chill, get my drink on, and get faded until whenever the fuck these niggas decided to leave. These niggas acted like the strip club was the only place to go. They could be at the strip club every night and it was like being at a theme park for them. I was just trying to get some money.

The waitress came back with our drinks, and my boy Dante started barking at her. I swear this nigga was on some other shit. He was drunk off his ass and stumbling. Not to mention that the waitress looked like she wanted to slap the piss out of him. This was exactly why I didn't wanna be in this muthafucka. I knew I would end up babysitting his ass.

I gave the waitress an apologetic look and slid her a $50 bill for having to deal with his crazy ass. She smiled and took the money licking her lips. She did have some soup coolers on her. But it took more than that to get my attention.

She walked off and Dante stood up watching her walk away. This one chick walked past and we all turned to look. She had more ass than K. Michelle, well the old K Michelle. That thang looked like it rippled when you smacked it. She was talking to this nigga and after making that thang jump, homeboy damn near jumped out of his seat to go to the back with her.

"Damn man. These females got it easy." I said.

"Hell yeah." Dante agreed taking a drink. "They in here getting all this money just because they got fat asses. Shit, they asses ain't throwing money at niggas like that."

"Oh hell nah." I laughed. "Bruh if a nigga was smacking her in the face with a dick, she complaining. They be begging us to strip and shit but want us to pay them to do it."

"That's because we got the power of the pussy," a stripper said walking up on us.

She looked at me and winked, and I gave her a little smile. I had to admit, she was bad.

"Yea and we end up paying for it." I said. "Well not me. I ain't paying for sex. I'm paying for you to leave."

The boys started cracking up and she smirked.

"Trust me, I don't get paid to leave. I get paid to stay."

She emphasized the last word and twirled around showing off her curves. I could see how she had niggas paying her to stay. But I just wasn't that nigga.

"Aye bruh heads up." Dre warned.

I looked up to see Dymond making a beeline to me and rolled my eyes.

"Did I interrupt something?" she hissed.

"Nope." I replied taking a drink.

"Nah girl just listening to these fools whine about how they can't get this money like us," the girl laughed.

"Uh huh." Dymond side-eyed her. "Well I was coming to tell you that they changed the rotation. They about to put that new girl on real quick. So you gotta go after her now."

"Cool," she said, turning around and hugging her customer. "I'll be right back baby."

He handed her some more money, and she switched off towards the back.

Dymond tried to put her arms around me to hug me but I pushed her off.

"Whatever," she said rolling her eyes. "I gotta go try to make some money."

She walked off and everybody was watching me.

"See why I said I ain't wanna come up in here?" I told Dre.

He laughed and took another shot ignoring me.

"Nigga take a shot and chill," he slurred.

I swear if he wasn't my cousin I would knock his midget ass out. He was at least five inches shorter than me and the nigga was getting a gut from that relationship weight. He killed me trying to check me but hiding from his baby mama.

The music switched up as we all stood around the bar and took shots together. Cardi B came blasting through the speakers, and I heard the DJ introducing one of the dancers.

"Yo is that a kid?" Dante asked squinting at the stage.

I looked up to see this light skin girl with a red wig on come out on the stage. She was tiny but it was her freckles that got my attention.

"Oh shit." I said.

"What's good?" Dre asked looking around instinctively.

"Yo, I think I know that girl." I told him watching her.

I walked off leaving them standing at the bar and headed to the stage so I could get a closer look. Maneuvering through the crowd of niggas, the closer that I got, I knew it was her ass.

This was the chic I had helped last week! Damn shorty was a stripper? I never would have guessed that shit.

"Who that?" Dante asked walking up behind me.

I watched her dancing on the pole and knew there was no way in hell that she was a regular at this shit. She looked nervous as fuck, but she was out there. She was doing this weird routine around the pole and spinning and doing the splits. It looked more like a cheerleader routine then stripping but dudes were throwing money and encouraging her.

I made my way through the small crowd and got close to the stage so she could see me. I pulled out a couple of bills and tossed them her way. She was moving around the stage and picking it up.

She looked good. She was wearing some lime green swimsuit looking outfit with fishnets and this weird ass red wig. I watched her in amusement as she went to each guy that gave her money and they were grabbing her and trying to pull her to them. She was trying to hide her fear as she took their money.

When she got to me, I pulled out a few more bills and held them up for her with a grin on my face.

"I see we meet again."

She squinted her eyes at me and when she realized who I was, her eyes bucked out of her head.

"Don't worry baby girl you good." I told her. "Why don't you come holla at me when you're done."

She looked like a deer in headlights she was so shocked. I turned and smiled and headed back to my boys who were watching to see what was going on.

"So you feeling strippers all of a sudden?" Dre snorted.

"Nah man." I told him grabbing a barstool. "So check this out. Last week, I was on my way to go see ole girl when I pulled up on this chick just walking down the street. Some niggas was tailing her ass bout to jack her and shit. That's the girl right there. But, she didn't look nothing like that. She was all bougie and spoiled. At least that's what I thought."

"Well shit, she must not be bougie working up in here." Dre laughed.

She was on stage still dancing to her second song.

"Yo that's the thing." I stressed. "Her ass was walking around with some goddamn Louis Vuitton luggage and shit not paying attention to what the fuck was going on. Her and her dude had got into it or some shit, I don't know if he put her out or if she left, but I had to take her to get a hotel room and shit."

I was watching her dance for the rest of her set, and almost busted out laughing when she practically ran off the stage. I remembered Dymond saying something to the other stripper about it being her first night.

I guess shit ain't work out with her and her nigga.

My curiosity was getting the best of me so I waited to see if she would come out. I sat and waited and eventually she made her way out from backstage. I got up and walked over to where she was standing by the bar. She had a bunch of thirsty ass niggas circling her but, she actually looked relieved when I came up.

"Hey," she said nervous.

"Wassup." I smiled.

A few of the niggas that was trying to get at her were sucking their teeth and watching. I wish one of these niggas would try to roll up. These niggas knew what it was.

"Didn't think I'd see you in here." I smirked.

"Yeah well, it wasn't necessarily the plan," she laughed grabbing her drink from the bartender and taking a big gulp.

Was she drinking soda? Wow. Yea she was on some other shit.

She looked shook. I kind of felt bad for her.

"So what's good with ya? You ever get in touch with your home-girl?" I asked making small talk.

"Yeah," she nodded quickly. "She came and got me the next morning. Thank you again for your help that night. Oh...here," she said reaching into her garter. "I told you I was going to pay you back."

"Yo you good." I laughed. "You in the strip club baby girl. You're supposed to *take* the money not give it."

"I know," she giggled wrinkling her nose. "But, you did me a solid. You didn't have to help me out and you did."

"Yo, what's with the red hair?" I asked changing the subject.

"Well...I mean... I didn't want anybody to recognize me," she answered.

"So you put on a bright red wig." I nodded trying not to laugh.

She frowned at my facial expression but started laughing herself.

"I know but, my best friend got a homegirl that works here. She told me to get a wig just in case somebody recognizes me or something," she explained. "To tell the truth though, I don't think the manager is gonna keep me on. I am WAY out of my element."

"You gotta do what you gotta do." I shrugged. "so what's your stage name?"

"You're going to laugh," she warned.

"What is it?" I asked.

"Ginger," she rushed.

"Yo, that is the whitest name." I laughed.

"Well I couldn't think of anything else," she whined. "The guy that hired me kept saying that I was a cute little redbone. And the only stripper names I knew were already taken so, I just said Ginger."

"There you are." I heard.

I turned around to see Dymond walking up.

The niggas standing around was all drooling over her as she made her way through.

Here we go.

I knew it was about to be some bullshit.

"I was looking for you," she sang. "I'm about to hit the stage."

She looked at Skyy and I could see it was about to be some bull shit.

"You're the new girl right?" She asked.

"Yeah." Skyy nodded.

"Oh okay. Well I'm Dymond."

"Skyy," she introduced herself putting her hand out.

Dymond looked at her and I could see nothing but evil.

"Well just a heads up Skyy," she started ignoring her gesture. "If the manager sees you standing around talking and the club got a bunch of money in it, he gonna send you home. He doesn't like having chicks standing around doing nothing so, you better get out there and show some ass."

"Oh wow I didn't know. Thanks," she thanked her.

Dymond ass was standing there with this fake smile on her face.

"No problem. That's what I'm here for."

Skyy had no clue how petty she was being.

"I'ma holla at you before I leave." I told her.

"Okay," she smiled putting her glass down.

She actually excused herself to make herself seen and Dymond dumb ass winked at me like I was going to be impressed or something.

All I could do was shake my head and go back to my boys.

This broad was delusional.

SKYY

"Hey Ginger! You did your thing out there girl!"

"Thanks." I replied fanning myself as Bella walked by.

I was backstage in the dressing room sitting in the chair. I was trying to get myself together after spending the last twenty minutes doing private dances and then getting up on the stage. I was hot! I was ready to go home but the club didn't close until like six in the morning. Plus I was making money!

It was my second night at the club, and I had already made close to $1,000. Clearly, it wasn't a lot for some of the girls that worked there, but for me it was. Some of these chicks were making over three grand a night and worked like four or five days a week. I could see why because they could do some amazing tricks with their body parts. I saw one girl make a champagne bottle disappear up her pussy. Ain't no way in hell could I do some shit like that. Still, $1,000 was well on my way to me getting my own place.

I looked around at some of the girls and noticed how comfortable they were with each other. They were walking around naked and touching each other comparing their asses and all that. My ass was changing in the bathroom because these chicks had me in my feelings!

60

My little ass was built like a stick. They asses was apple bottoms but mine was a plum. Tierra's homegirl Bella had gone to the DR to get a Brazilian butt lift and to get some new titties and was planning on going back to get her waist snatched in some more. I was glad I didn't have those problems. I had a little shape to me but not like theirs.

My mind drifted back to Remy. I thought I would be more nervous with him being there but I wasn't. I did realize that his ass didn't take the money that I tried to give him. I didn't want to be a charity case to him. No. He was going to take this money. If he wouldn't take it from me then maybe I could give it to one of his boys or something to give to him.

Dymond walked in, smiling when she saw me and headed over in my direction.

"What's happening girl?" She said happy. "Everything going good with you?"

"Yeah it's going okay." I told her. "I don't know if I can do this though. It just feels weird."

"Oh girl you'll get used to it," she assured me. "I was nervous as hell my first week."

"Really?" I asked not convinced.

"No for real," she nodded. "Trust me, it gets so much better. It's second nature now because I've been doing it for so long."

"How long have you been dancing?" I pressed.

"Like four years," she told me. "When I first started working here, I couldn't do none of the shit that I can do now."

I found that hard to believe. I had watched Dymond on stage and she was amazing. It was like watching one of those videos with her. She would climb to the top of the pole and then come down into the splits. She was doing butterfly tricks and all kinds of stuff. If she was ever nervous, I couldn't tell.

"You'll get the hang of it," she promised. "If you want, I can teach you some stuff."

Dymond seemed real cool. All those rumors that I had heard about strippers being cut throat and stuff like that wasn't really something I was seeing. She was helpful and nice.

"I appreciate it." I told her. "I'm trying to make enough money so that I can get my own place."

"I feel you," she said reaching over and grabbing a lighter from her purse. "You smoke?"

"Nah I'm good." I declined. She lit her blunt and started smoking. "I'ma give you some advice though."

"What's up?" I asked her as I put on some lotion and got some contact from her weed.

"Be careful with some of these niggas," she warned. "These broads in here is shady as hell. They'll smile in your face and act like everything is cool and be plotting on the nigga that you trying to get money from. If you turn your back on a dude, I guarantee you another broad gonna to be up in his face trying to get in his pockets. If you see a dude that got money, do whatever you can to get his ass," she advised taking another hit from her blunt.

I nodded my head in understanding trying not to cough from the smoke. I had already witnessed some of what she was talking about. I saw first hand how one dancer would be talking to a customer and then as soon as she got up, another chick would come and swoop right in.

"Just be careful is all I'm saying," she added.

"I appreciate it." I thanked her.

She nodded and took another drag before putting her blunt out.

"Let me get my ass back on this floor. I still got to make another $400 by the end of the night and it's almost three in the morning," she rattled off. "You might want to get out there too. It's a couple of niggas that came in with some heavy pockets out there."

"Cool." I smiled standing up and making myself cute.

Looking in the mirror, I realized that Remy was right. This wig did look stupid. I can't believe I had actually wore that shit. The first thing I'm going to do in the morning was get a different wig. I was glad that I had bought one because as much as these girls and these customers be smoking, there was no way I was going home with my hair smelling like weed every night. Plus, I wanted to get some new outfits anyway. I was wearing bathing suits while these girls were walking around in g-strings and heels. I looked real basic. Maybe I could ask Dymond to help me with that.

Once I was satisfied with my looks, I walked back out onto the floor and saw a couple of new bodies. It had cleared out a little bit so I could see actual faces. Taking a couple of deep breaths and trying to get my confidence together I looked around for somebody that I could use to achieve my goal.

One guy was sitting in the corner and kept his eyes on me the whole time. He looked real nerdy, so I figured he would be an easy target. I tried to switch my hips as I walked over to him and smiled.

"Hey handsome." I greeted sitting down next to him and smiling seductively. "I'm Ginger."

He fidgeted and looked down at his hands.

"Herman," he whispered.

Yep. My assumption was right. Even his name screamed nerd.

"Have you been here before?" I asked making small talk.

"A few times," he answered not looking at me.

He was wearing khaki pants and a polo shirt. His body language was telling me he was an accountant or personal assistant or something like that.

"I haven't seen you before," he observed.

"Yeah I know." I nodded. "I'm new. This is my second night here."

"Oh okay."

We both sat there looking awkward as hell and I was starting to feel like I was wasting my time. I looked to see a lot of guys making their way towards the stage when Dymond walked out. Even I was hypnotized by her. She was fucking gorgeous. Some song by the Migos that I had never heard of came blasting out through the speakers and every dude in there went crazy.

She started swirling around the pole twerking her ass, and I was jealous as hell. I wish I could move my ass like that!

"I'll be right back baby." I said to the nerd.

I was feeling thirsty all of a sudden. I went over to the bar to get me something to drink. I needed to get some liquid courage and quick so I could convince this guy to do a dance with me.

"So how's it going?"

Remy popped up at the bar next to me.

"Hey." I smiled. "It's going."

"Yeah? I peeped you sitting over there with Urkel," he said.

I flipped him the finger and he smiled.

Did I notice a dimple? How did I miss that before?

"So what you drinking?" he asked.

"Patron." I answered.

He nodded in approval at my response and motioned for one of the bartenders who rushed over. She took a few seconds and gave him four shot glasses. I immediately grabbed two and took them to the head damn near burning a hole in my chest.

"Damn girl," he watched in admiration. "Take it easy."

"Why?" I flirted. "Because I'm a girl?"

"Nah because your ass weigh like 90 pounds soaking wet," he laughed.

I rolled my eyes and placed the glass back on the countertop. The liquor was already working its magic on me. I was warm as hell and had started to relax a little bit.

"So I got a question for you." I said tapping him on the chest feeling his abs.

Damn that shit was rock hard.

"What's up?" He asked.

"So, you been here this whole time and I haven't seen you up on any girl except Dymond." I mentioned.

"And?" He said.

"So, is that like your favorite dancer or something? Or your... girlfriend?"

He gave me an amused look.

"I don't do girlfriends," he told me with a straight face.

"You make it sound like it's a job or something." I frowned.

"Pretty much," he shrugged. "You gotta put in a lot of work, you don't get paid, and usually there's some type of workplace drama. So I just don't do it."

"So then if she's not your girlfriend or anything like that, then how come you haven't been up on any other girl?"

"Cause that ain't my thing," he replied taking a shot. He seemed real nonchalant and cocky about the matter. "I ain't got to pay some chick to dance up on me. For what? I can beat my meat at home."

"Well damn." I laughed in surprise. "So then why come at all?"

He shrugged and took the last shot.

"The fellas wanted to chill and meet up with some folks."

I looked in the direction of the two guys I had seen him with earlier surrounded by a bunch of females. Suddenly I had an idea.

I grabbed him by the hand and attempted to pull him towards one of the rooms. Clearly, he didn't budge because he was much bigger than me.

"Yo what you doing?"

"You're going to get a dance from me." I said. "I need the practice and I have a feeling that you'll be brutally honest."

"I told you, I don't pay no chick to make her ass clap," he argued.

"Who said you were paying?"

He actually looked surprised for a second.

"You thought that I wasn't paying attention earlier when I tried to give you your money back, huh?" I asked. "Me giving you this private dance will be my way of paying you back and practicing at the same time. So, come on."

He shook his head and looked like he was about to argue, but I interrupted him.

"Please..." I said giving him a little pout.

He smirked and finally agreed.

"Aight fuck it," he caved. "You just wasting your money though."

"Technically..." I said. "I'm wasting yours."

I took his hand and led him to the room. A few of the girls noticed and eyeballed me. Dymond was right. They were jealous but I wasn't about to let someone stop my money. I was going to take her advice and get my money. I was not about to let anybody stop my coins.

We went into the room and he flopped down on the couch. I tried to mimic what I had seen other girls do. I mounted him trying to grind my hips in a circular motion. It was a little awkward at first, and he sat with this sarcastic look on his face but, I just closed my eyes and let the music take over.

Sex With Me by R. Kelly came on, and I pretended that I was doing just that. Sexing Remy. I wasn't going to lie and say that I wasn't attracted to him. He was fine as hell, but he wasn't my type.

I moved my hips and swayed to the beat of the song turning and putting my ass all up on him. He put his hands around my hips and I just let myself go. My body was enjoying the feel of him against me. His face was so close to me that I could feel his breath against my skin.

When the song stopped, I opened my eyes to see him staring at me with this lustful gaze. I was feeling a little tingle in between my legs as we stared at each other. His lips were juicy and he licked them making me damn near lose it.

Get up Sky! I was telling myself.

If I didn't, my pussy was about to start purring like a house cat.

"So, how'd I do?" I said standing up quickly.

I was trying to fix my top when I noticed the dick print in his pants. I guess he must have noticed too but he didn't give a fuck.

"What you think?" he said motioning to it. "You did your thing."

Good gawd that thing looked thick.

"Really?" I said hopeful. "Cause I never even took off my top."

I didn't realize until the song was over that I was so into the dance, I never actually stripped.

I could see that he hadn't paid attention either because he finally looked at me with a perplexed look.

"Yo you didn't," he replied. "So I guess that means you owe me another one."

I grinned and headed towards the door.

"Maybe later."

I left him sitting on the couch and rushed to the dressing room. I had to get away from his ass. My panties were soaked. I damn sure didn't expect that to happen.

One of the girls that had been watching me earlier walked in my path with an attitude and stopped me.

"Excuse me." I said trying to go around her.

"You should've excused yourself before you took Remy into the champagne room," she growled.

She walked past bumping into me and I turned around confused.

"What?" I said confused.

She kept walking like she didn't hear me and I tried to figure out what the hell had just happened.

What the hell does that mean? What did I do?

I looked around for Dymond to ask her what was going on but couldn't see her anywhere. It was winding down in there so I assumed she had either left or was doing a dance.

I walked in the room to my bag to change outfits.

"Where's my bag?" I mumbled looking around my station.

It was nowhere to be found. Girls were coming in and out, and I was trying not to bother them, but I needed my stuff. I walked into the bathroom and noticed a purple bag in the corner. The bathroom was filthy and the floor was covered with lashes, old toilet tissue, tracks, and everything you could think of. It was what was in the toilet that caught my attention. A few of my outfits were covered in piss and shit.

Somebody actually took a shit on my clothes! What kind of fucked up mess is this?

I looked up at the girls that were back in the room with me and I remembered the girl that had just stopped me outside.

Did she do this shit?

Some of the girls were watching and pointing and laughing.

"Dymond told you don't fuck with her man," one of the girls name Kat said walking past. "She tried to warn you but you went and took her nigga into the champagne room. Should have known better."

She walked out like it was nothing.

I wanted to break all the way down but I continued to be calm.

Bitches was really pissing and shitting on people's stuff over some dick? All I did was dance on him.

This was only further proof that I could not be in a place like this. I was about to lose all the money I made on bail because I was ready to fuck somebody up.

REMY

"So what the fuck was that?" Dymond spat as soon as I came around the corner.

"What the fuck you talking about?" I huffed.

As if I didn't already know.

"I'm talking about you in the champagne room with that little skinny ass bitch!" She accused. She was getting loud and everybody could hear her which only hyped her up more. "Sooo all the times you come up to the club, and I'm helping you get customers but you spitting that bullshit about how you don't spend money and then I see you taking that bitch back there? What? She taking product for you now? Really? That's what you do?"

She was putting her finger in my face and shit, and I don't normally even think about hitting women but she was about to catch a fade right here in the middle of the fucking club. This the exact reason why I don't fuck with these kind of broads man. They get too emotional. You give them a little bit of dick and they lose their damn mind.

When I saw Skyy coming up behind her, I knew it was about to be some shit. Skyy looked upset and I would bet my last dollar that Dymond had something to do with it. Of course she saw that I was looking at her and I didn't think it was possible but, she got even louder.

"Woowww!" she laughed all loud clapping and shit. "So you trying to fuck her now?"

She was getting all in my face and poking me in the forehead and shit. See this how bitches get hit and then wanna cry victim.

Skyy saw what was going on and turned to head back to the dressing room. I didn't blame her. This bitch was off her rocker. Like she was still going off not even realizing I wasn't paying attention to her.

"Yo, you got to be the dumbest bitch you know that?" I spoke no longer giving a fuck.

She finally shut the hell up long enough for her mouth to fly open, like she was actually surprised I was coming at her.

"What? I ain't speaking loud enough for you?" I smirked. "See I tried to be nice to your ass despite you acting stupid. I told you I wasn't tryna fuck with you like that. You knew I wasn't tryna wife you. You were just a fuck. Get that shit through your head yo. I don't give a fuck about you. I never did shit for you other than fuck you. So all this questioning shit, you can go on with that."

This time I was in her face and I didn't give a fuck. Muthafuckas was standing around watching the shit, some of them trying not to laugh and some of them looking nervous like they thought some shit would go down. She looked like she wanted to run away and cry, but I wasn't done. Not after the way she had just tried to clown me. Nah, shawty was going to get exactly what she deserved.

"Oh what you embarrassed now?" I smiled.

I peeped security in the corner coming over, but I wasn't worried. Wasn't nobody bout to hit her ass. I just wanted to make her look as stupid as she was acting.

"Dymond go to the dressing room," he told her.

"Nah you good." I told him satisfied that she was feeling dumb. "I'm bout to be out. I got shit to do."

She waited until we started to leave to pop off again.

"Fuck you and that bitch!" she called out when I was almost to the door. "I was tired of fucking your little dick ass anyway."

"Mann please." I laughed turning around. "With as much of my nut that you swallow, everybody in here knows your breath be smelling like dick bitch. Shidd I'm surprised your knees don't have dark spots as much as you be on em."

Niggas was hollering laughing and her ass was hot.

"Yeah whatever!" She yelled out stomping off. "Nigga you can't fuck no way! Can't stay in the pussy for more than five minutes."

"That's because I was tired of smelling that shit. Gah damn pussy smelling like ear wax and boiled cabbage." I yelled back.

It was like a comedy club the way everyone exploded in laughter. I walked over to the manager to dap him up. I brought work for all them hoes in there so I knew they wouldn't do shit to me. They would get rid of her ass long before I stopped coming through. I tossed him a couple of bills for my tab as he apologized for the shit and me and my boys finally headed out.

"Damn my nigga." Dre laughed. "Earwax though?"

"Man, y'all know I just be shooting the shit." I replied. "But fuck that bitch man, I'm tryna go get something to eat cause a nigga hungry as shit."

"Hell yeah. I can rock with that."

We were headed to the truck when I saw Skyy standing under the awning on the side of the building holding her purse. She was wiping her eyes from crying. She had this tee shirt on over her clothes. She saw me and turned her back. I tossed the keys to Dante so him and Dre could go ahead and get in the truck while I figured out what the hell was going on. Dre shook his head but said nothing. Damn. Once again, I found myself wanting to help her.

This girl just couldn't be this naïve.

"Yo, are you just a magnet for danger or something?" I questioned.

"What?" She sniffed turning to me.

What the hell was she crying for?

"You good?" I asked.

"No, I'm not thanks to you!" She snapped.

71

"The fuck I do?"

"Well Mr. *I don't have a girlfriend but you in there arguing with a chic that's put all y'all business out there*, all of my clothes are cut up and dumped in the toilet thanks to you," she told me. "So that's why I'm standing out here with a shirt on because I don't have anything else to wear. I'm waiting on my Uber."

"Annnnd you really gonna take a Uber dressed like that?" I said looking at her like she was crazy. "Can you say human trafficking? Good luck with that shit."

This girl was literally standing out here with a t-shirt that barely covered her small ass, some stripper heels, and a garter. She had taken that dusty ass wig off at least, but she was an easy target.

"I already checked. My Uber driver is a woman thank you, so I'll be fine."

"Oh my bad, I forgot women drivers ain't in the human trafficking shit." I said. I was being sarcastic as hell because she was living in a fairytale or some shit. "Look, if it's that big of a deal, why don't you just let me give you a ride? It's not like I haven't done it before."

"No!" She refused. "I don't need any more of your crazy girlfriends after me. Talking to you got my shit fucked up. What, you tryna have your girl set me on fire next?"

"Yo first off, I told you that's not my girl." I checked her. "That was just some chick that I was fucking with."

She looked at me with these wide eyes, and I almost wanted to laugh.

"And you didn't think I needed to know that?"

"You ain't ask." I shrugged. "You asked me if that was my girl and I told you no. I told you I don't do relationships."

"Yeah, well clearly she does," she hissed rolling her neck with a whole bunch of unnecessary attitude. "I swear you men are dumb as hell. You know that doesn't work like that right? Any chick that tell you that she can handle being a booty buddy is lying. You gone put it down, and then she goes crazy and starts getting territorial."

I had to give it to her. She was right. That's exactly what happened.

"I don't know what I was thinking about doing this shit," she sighed. "I can't go back in there."

"Why?"

"Hello!" She yelled. "She cut my shit and threw it in the toilet!"

"Okay." I said not really seeing the big deal. "So I'll get you some new ones."

"And give her something else to get pissed off about?" She pressed looking at me crazy. "Are you just trying to see me fight or something? Cause… I may be small, but I will scrap if I have to. Especially when I need this money."

I smiled at her attitude. She actually sounded confident. This little bougie suburban chick seemed like she had a little bit of hood in her.

"Well like I said, I'm not letting your ass get in the Uber. So you might as well get in the truck with me. I can take you to get some clothes, take you to your friend's house or wherever. But you're not taking an Uber." I told her.

She looked at my truck and saw Dante and Dre sitting in it.

"So a ride with three dudes is better?" she snorted. "You talk about you don't want me to take a Uber cause something may happen but you want me to get in the car with three niggas?"

I almost laughed out loud because it sounded like she put the 'ER' on the end of that shit.

"Nah I'm good." She declined.

"Trust me lil mama I ain't worried about you and neither is my boys. Dante got a girl at home, and Dre fucking wit one of the chics in the club already." I informed her.

"Oh my God," she rolled her eyes.

"You ain't got nothing to worry about." I promised her. "Did I do anything to you last time?"

"No." she shivered.

She was standing and holding herself. I knew she was cold.

"Let's just get in. If you want, I'll drop them off first."

She looked around and looked at her phone again.

"You might as well. Cause if you stand out here, I'm pretty sure

Dymond crazy ass will eventually find out that you're still here. And I can't hit no female. At least not in front of everybody." I joked.

She looked at me and sighed, giving in and following me to my truck.

"If you want, I got a sweatshirt in the back of my truck." I offered. "It ain't much, but it'll cover you up at least until we get to where you're going."

"Thanks," she said giving me a small smile.

I opened the trunk to find the oversized sweatshirt. When she put it on, it swallowed her up, but I could tell she felt better.

"Meet the boys." I introduced as we hopped in.

"Hey," she greeted giving them a small smile.

"Yo what up," they replied. Dre was on his phone no doubt texting his girl some lie as to where he was. That nigga was always doing some shit he ain't have no business doing and always getting caught. I don't get why he didn't just stay single. Shit, he acted like he was anyway.

"Aye change of plans. I'ma go ahead and drop y'all off first." I told Dante and Dre.

"Aight that's straight." Dante spoke up.

I could see him checking her out. I don't know why the fuck that shit bothered me but it did. And shawty was just clueless to the whole thing because she was on her phone. I headed to his crib and dropped both of them off letting them know I would link up with them later.

"Where am I taking you, to your homegirl house?" I asked.

"Yeah," she nodded.

"Aight. I think I still got the address in my GPS."

I opened up Waze to get it out my driving history and headed her way.

"So how'd you make out"? I asked killing the silence.

"I did okay I guess. Well...up until my stuff was destroyed," she rolled her eyes towards me. "I made more than what I thought I would though. Hopefully I can get more next time."

"I thought you said you weren't going back?" I recalled.

"I did say that, but right now it's the only way that I'm gonna be able to make some quick money," she told me. "I don't really have any experience with anything else aside from when I was working at my ex-boyfriend's father's firm. But once he and I got together, I stopped working."

"Oh okay. I gotcha." I nodded my head. "Well I'm sure you got a lot of niggas in there tryna get at you."

"I guess," she shrugged.

We drove in silence, and my stomach growled loud enough for her to hear it.

"Hungry much?" she laughed.

"Yeah a lil bit. I was actually headed to go get something to eat." I told her.

"See now I feel bad. I shoulda just took the Uber," she huffed.

"Nah you straight." I said. "You just gonna go with me."

"Umm... no I'm not!" she argued.

"Why not?"

"Hello? Maybe cause all I'm wearing is a T-shirt and a sweatshirt and some heels? I look like somebody's crazy ass crackhead cousin right now," she pointed out.

"All right so we'll stop at like Walmart or something and I'll get you some pants and some sneakers." I told her.

"Remy..."

"Come on I'm hungry." I persuaded her. "Besides we right here by the IHOP anyway and there's a Walmart down the street."

"I'm just going to assume that you're not used to having women tell you no huh?" she said looking at me.

I took my attention off the traffic for a second to meet her gaze.

"Basically." I told her. "I thought you would have seen that after tonight."

"Somebody is really feeling themselves," she snorted.

"Got to. I look good." I grinned.

And so do you. I wanted to say.

Even though she wasn't the type of chick that I was used to, she definitely was attractive. She was the exact opposite of what I was used to dealing with. These chicks would jump at the chance to do whatever I say. That's why it was so easy to fuck them. But shawty was different. She was argumentative. She seemed real sure of herself but at the same time she had this whole naive shit that just didn't understand how the world worked.

I pulled into the Walmart and made her give me her size. I bolted inside to get her some sweats while she called her roommate. I was running around Walmart like a kid looking for condoms on prom night. I didn't realize it until after I was going through self-checkout with her stuff that I was nervous.

Why the fuck was I nervous? I ain't even know her like that. But, part of me wanted to.

Nah man. I convinced myself.

Fuck the fact that I was thinking about sliding up in her. I wasn't about to fall though. Nah. Not the kid.

SKYY

"Did you want a refill on your drink?" The waitress asked.

"Nah I'm good, thank you." I told her.

"Aye let me get some more though." Remy said pushing his cup to the edge.

"Alright," she smiled at him. "Sit tight. I'll be right back."

She walked off and he turned his attention back to me. We were sitting across from each other talking and laughing after pulling up at IHOP to get something to eat. The flow of the conversation was going so well between us that we never noticed how the early morning sun began to slowly rise. After he dropped his boys off, Remy had taken me to Walmart to get some sweats and a pair of cheap slide ons. Afterwards, we ended up here. I had spent the majority of the time monopolizing the conversation telling Remy about my situation with Malachi and going back over how it all started before he put me out. I also told him how Malachi had been calling me non-stop for the last two weeks since I had been gone and threatening to cut my phone off. I had joked about sleeping with the next nigga to make him mad and of course Remy was quick to volunteer. As fine as he was looking, I was tempted to take him up on it too. But right now it was other shit stopping that from happening.

Despite the fact that I barely knew him, he was actually a pretty good listener. I told him about how Malachi had basically saved me and brought me up off the streets after my mother passed. I couldn't believe I had gotten so comfortable talking to him. Of course, this was only the second time that I had seen him since meeting him, but Remy actually turned out to be pretty cool. I had gotten to know a little about him, like the fact that he didn't have any kids. I knew that he was a drug dealer. He never outright said it, but I wasn't stupid either. I had seen drug dealers around my mama all the time growing up, so I knew what was up.

Low key it irked me a little. I barely knew this nigga from Adam, but the fact that he was just slinging this shit and not giving a fuck got under my skin. Maybe it's because of what happened to my mom I don't know, but that shit just bugged the fuck out of me. I heard Dymond saying something about her bringing him customers when they had gotten into it at the club earlier. I was just going to leave it alone. Besides, I didn't know him like that. And, even though he was hustling, he had helped me out so I would drop it.

The waitress came back with a pitcher of iced tea, pouring it for him and low-key flirting. I watched him pour damn near half the sugar dispenser in his glass.

"Okay so your ass is gonna end up with diabetes." I joked.

"I ain't drinking that white people shit," he told me.

I laughed at him because I knew it was true. We were at IHOP and basically everybody that worked there with the exception of our waitress was white and elderly.

"See, that's why you gotta go to Shoney's." I told him. "That place is good as hell."

"Well, next time I'll take you there," he said taking a sip of his drink giving me a look.

"Next time?" I said my eyebrows shooting up.

"My bad," he dismissed.

I stared at him for a second, but he avoided eye contact and kept drinking his tea.

"So what's up with you and Dymond?" I asked switching the subject and killing the dead air.

"Ain't shit up," he answered bluntly. "She and I have an understanding. She just think she my girl and shit."

"Uh huh," I nodded slowly. "And you don't think you have anything to do with that?"

"What you mean?" He asked putting a forkful of his omelet in his mouth.

"I mean, you know how y'all are." I tried to explain.

"Y'all who?" he pressed.

"Y'all men!" I said with a roll of my eyes. "You guys like to meet a chick, sweet talk her and have her thinking that she's the only one when you know she's not. Then you have the girl all in her feelings thinking that y'all feel the same way." I started. "But the whole time you just trying to fuck."

"Nah. I don't need to lie or lead no woman on," he said. "I want what I want. I put my shit out there. And Dymond knew what was up. I told her I wasn't trying to have no girl from the start. She just got comfortable. That's on her."

"So you don't have any feelings for her?" I asked curious.

"Nah," he shook his head. "Especially not now. I can't have no chick like that."

"Why? Because she's a stripper?" I pushed.

"That's part of it," he confessed licking his lips. Damn them shits looked soft as hell. "I ain't tryna have a bunch of niggas looking at my girl shake her ass and shit. If I got a girl, she ain't doing no shit like that. She won't need to anyway because I'm going to take care of her."

"Well maybe the woman doesn't want a man to just simply take care of her." I argued. "Maybe she wants to do things for herself and not have someone doing shit for her just to rub it in her face."

He looked at me and frowned.

"My bad. I was thinking about my own situation." I admitted. "I told you, that's what happened with me and Malachi. I got comfortable with letting him take care of me and just sat at home playing the good little girlfriend and look how that ended up."

"I feel you," he said. "But your situation and hers is different. Trust me, she wants me to take care of her. She the type of chick that gets off on bragging and shit about what she got and what nigga is giving it to her. I'm low-key with mine. I don't want everybody in my business. If I got a girl, she gone be straight. But just don't be bringing attention my way. Cause when you bring attention you bring trouble."

"Well, I know with what you do, clearly attention or trouble isn't a good thing." I mentioned with a hint of sarcasm.

He smirked and finished the rest of his iced tea.

"Trouble is never a good thing in anything you do. It's trouble," he shrugged.

"Ha ha." I sneered. He had this cockiness that confused the shit out of me. A part of me wanted to smack him and tell him about himself, but the other part of me was turned on. "So I take it that your boys that were with you earlier are in the same line of...work?"

"Yeah. We got a business," he told me.

"A business?" I asked. "Interesting."

"What?" He said.

"So that's what they call it now?" I pressed.

"You asking a lot of questions," he observed.

"I'm a curious person." I shrugged.

"Yeah well you know what they say, curiosity killed the cat."

"True." I conceded. "You're right. It ain't none of my business."

We both sat there in an awkward silence as he played with the straw in his cup. The waitress came over and he asked for the check.

"I should probably be getting home." I finally spoke. "I know Tierra is probably spazzing the fuck out. Well, at least she will be once she wakes up and notices that I'm not there."

"Aight," he grunted before getting up from his seat and motioning for me to follow him to the front so that he could pay. He looked back at me over his shoulder briefly, "If you don't mind me asking, what made you start working in the club? Looking at you, I would never peg you as the type to be dancing at a spot like that for tips. You seem kind of...bougie."

"Honestly I really needed to make some money." I told him. "I had Malachi taking care of me and now I don't. I want to do things for myself and not have somebody doing it because they want to remind me that they did it. I wanna get shit on my own. But truthfully, being up in there, especially after tonight, I don't know if that's going to be a good look. I just know I need to do something. I can't just be sitting at Tierra's house. And I'm not going back to Malachi."

"Yea that ain't gone be a good look," he agreed. "Cause that ain't gone do nothing but show that nigga you weak. And you don't really strike me as the type to be as weak as you were making yourself sound."

"I'm not." I urged. "I just gave up a lot to be with him. I thought that because he was taking care of me and all of that, that it would just be easier to just do what he wanted. But, I just don't want to live like that anymore. I want to go to school. I want to get my degree. I want to do something with my life."

"Then do it," he said as we walked out.

"That's so much easier said than done." I sighed. "I gotta get money. I gotta pay bills and rent and all that. I mean, Tierra don't mind me staying with her and everything but I gotta be able to take care of myself. I know it sounds stupid but I need to prove him wrong. Shit, I gotta prove myself wrong. I got to show myself that I can do this."

"I feel you," he said.

I looked over and saw that he had this strange smile on his face.

"What?" I asked.

"Nothing," he said unlocking the truck. "Just sound real different from what I'm used to hearing on some real shit. I wish I could meet more females like you."

"Yeah too bad I'm just a stripper huh?" I reminded him.

He looked but didn't say anything and I hopped in the truck. I don't know why he was getting to me but he was. I knew he was fucking Dymond so I couldn't understand why I was tripping so much.

He hopped in and cranked the truck.

"You good?"

"Yeah." I told him. "Just a little tired."

"Well I live right down the street," he told me. "Why don't you just come kick it with me at the crib? You can take my room if you want. I'll sleep on the couch. I mean at least that way you can get some sleep and not have to worry about waking up your homegirl."

"I should be okay." I quickly declined. "Besides, she sleeps like a rock. So I don't think she'll hear me come in."

"Aight," he yawned.

I definitely wasn't about to tell him that if I went to his house that I would end up bouncing on that dick. I needed to get away from him fast.

"But I really appreciate it." I thanked him trying to recover. "I mean, for everything. You've been really helpful. I never would have thought that somebody like you would help me."

"Oh why, cause I'm a drug dealer?" he mocked.

I side eyed his ass but I wasn't going to say anything rude. After all, I was still in the truck and wasn't quite to my friend's house just yet.

"I didn't mean it like that." I told him. "It's just that...you look real hard. Like you have this whole *I don't give a fuck* demeanor about you. Like I saw how you went off on Dymond at the club and every-thing. It kind of seems like you don't really respect women too much. So for you to help me not once...but twice? Yeah, that's a little shocking."

"Damn," he burst out laughing. "Sounds like I'm a monster."

"Your perception." I shrugged.

"Well your perception is wrong," he argued.

I just nodded my head. I wasn't trying to argue. I just wanted to sleep.

I noticed that we weren't going in the direction of Tierra's house.

"Where are you going?" I asked.

"I told you I'm going to the house," he said.

"Yeah and I told you to take me home."

"Why you acting like you don't want to go home with me?" He

said. He pulled up at a stoplight and stared at me. "I know you want to."

The way that he was looking at me, hell yea I did! I swear my pussy literally screamed *'yes we wanna go bitch'*.

"And how do I know that you ain't tryna kidnap me or no shit like that." I smiled a little.

"Can't kidnap the willing," he winked turning the corner.

I didn't even have shit else to say. I just rode in silence. Was I really about to go home with this nigga? I guess so because a few minutes later we were pulling up to the parking lot of his apartment complex.

"You stay in an apartment?" I asked shocked.

"Yep," he nodded.

I was kind of thrown off with that.

"How you a drug dealer and you stay in an apartment?"

"I told you, I don't need everybody in my business," he said

I followed him upstairs and was quite impressed once we got inside. He had a nice little spot.

"Well this just screams bachelor pad." I joked.

"What you mean?" He asked.

"Black leather couch? Big screen TV? Ashtray on the living room table with smoked blunts. Empty beer bottles and shit." I pointed out. "Yeah. Looks like some stuff I would see on Love & Hip Hop or one of them shows."

I flopped down on the couch and watched as he tried to straighten up.

"You want something to drink or something?" he asked.

"Nah I'm good." I told him.

I watched him moving around and after a few minutes, he came and sat down.

"You know I normally don't do this right?" I said. He burst out laughing and I looked at him like he was crazy. "What the hell is so funny?"

"Yo, you know how many girls say that shit? *You know I normally don't do this right*," he mocked. "Them be the main freaks."

"Well I ain't them." I snapped. "And like I said, I don't normally do this. In fact I have never done this because unlike you I was actually in a relationship."

"What makes you think I wasn't in a relationship?" he asked taking off his Timbs.

"I don't know." I sighed. "Maybe the fact that you fuck random strippers."

"Well it wasn't always like that," he mumbled.

His face changed and it looked like he had kind of zoned out for a second.

"What does that mean?" I asked.

"Nothing."

"No tell me." I pressed.

"Damn why is it that y'all just can't leave shit the fuck alone?" He snapped.

I was thrown off by his sudden outburst. His entire mood had just changed and I didn't know why.

"Yea so…I'm just gonna call for an Uber and go." I said slowly.

I pulled out my phone fast and pulled up my Uber app. I didn't know what the hell was going on but the way he had flipped out just now was weird. I ordered my Uber and got my purse. I'd wait outside if I had to. I was standing up to leave when he finally spoke.

"My bad," he apologized rubbing his hand over his face. "I just don't really tell a lot of people about what happened."

"Well, you ain't gotta worry about telling me." I said walking towards the door. "My Uber will be here in six minutes."

"She was killed," he said as I opened the door.

"Huh?" I said turning around confused.

"My girl, she was killed," he repeated.

I just kind of stood there awkward not really knowing what to say.

"Her name was Nikki. We had been together for a minute. We went to college and everything together," he started.

"You were in college?" I asked walking back over to him. He smirked at the question and gave me a look. "I'm sorry." I quickly apologized.

"Nah it's cool," he dismissed. "But yeah I was. I wasn't always a dope boy. We were at Johnson C Smith together and she was pregnant with our daughter. But then one day I was in class and she was on her way to the store. Some drunk fool ran a red light and shit and knocked into her. They took her to the hospital but...she didn't make it. And it fucked me up."

He stopped and I placed my hand on his arm trying to comfort him.

"So ever since then I told myself I wouldn't be in a relationship. I ain't tryna be going through the motions and all that."

"Damn." I whispered sitting back down on the couch. "I'm sorry."

"It's cool," he shrugged. "It ain't like you knew. I ain't really mean to snap at you like that or whatever."

"It's okay." I assured him. My Uber beeped notifying me that it was outside and I looked at him concerned. "Are you gonna be okay?"

"Yea I'm straight," he told me looking up at the ceiling. "I mean, you ain't gotta leave or nothing. I mean, you can if you want to but...I didn't mean to snap like that and make you wanna leave."

I looked at my phone for a minute before I cancelled my ride. I didn't want to leave him here like this. I could tell that it was hurting him. Hearing him tell me that, I did feel bad for him. That was some heavy shit.

"How long ago was it?"

"Three years," he said still looking up at the ceiling. "Shit is crazy man."

I sat there looking at and feeling horrible for him.

"Remy, I—I don't know what to say. I'm so sorry."

I felt a lump in my throat and swallowed hard.

"It ain't like it's some shit I just go around talking about," he told me.

Seeing the pain in his face reminded me of the pain that I had been feeling for years when my mother died.

"Trust me I know what you're going through." I spoke taking his hand in mine. "It's not something that you can just get over so fast or so easy."

"Facts," he nodded.

I leaned back on the couch and realized that we were still holding hands. He looked down and I unclasped my hand from his.

"Yea, I think I'm bout to lay down," he said. "Come on I'ma show you where you sleeping."

"Okay." I yawned standing up and following behind him.

He lead me down the hallway and into his room. Thank God it didn't look anything like the living room did otherwise my ass would be ordering another Uber and getting the hell out of here.

"It ain't like no little nut spots on the sheets or anything is it?" I teased looking at the all black sheets.

Typical. I was serious though. My eyes were scanning for nut stains. I wish I had a black light.

"Ha, ha, ha very funny," he snorted. "But no."

"Okay. Just making sure I don't need to sleep on top of the covers." I laughed.

"Whatever," he rolled his eyes.

"Well can I get some towels for the shower?" I asked.

"Oh yea my bad," he said looking at me weird. "There should be some in the closet. The bathroom is down that way."

"Okay cool." I yawned.

"I'm going to be out on the couch," he announced.

"All right." I smiled. "You okay?"

I noticed that his face was still kind of sad.

"Yeah I'm straight," he nodded before he walked out of his room and back towards the living room.

I watched him walk down the hall before heading in the opposite direction. I walked to the bathroom and turned on the shower so that I could wash up and go to sleep. It had been a crazy day and I was still trying to get over the fact that Dymond's psycho ass put my shit in the fucking toilet. I couldn't prove that it was her, but I knew it was her.

Clearly Remy's ass was trouble from jump. That dick had to be some serious shit for a bitch to do something like that. Like homeboy had that big dick. I wondered how good it really was. I remembered how good it felt up against me earlier that night. Thank God I was in the shower because my pussy was soaking wet thinking about it. My fingers found their way to my pussy and I closed my eyes letting them massage my clit while I imagined Remy's tongue on me.

Damn I wanted this nigga bad! Yea I needed to take my ass to sleep before my hormones got the better of me.

I finally finished my shower after another ten minutes of thinking about Remy and playing with my pussy. I wrapped a towel around me and stepped out of the shower.

"Shit." I whispered realizing that I didn't have a change of clothes.

I was going to have to put on what I got from Walmart which was fine. I walked into the bedroom and there was an oversized t-shirt lying on the bed.

"I figured you'd need that." I heard come from behind me and jumped out of my skin.

"Damn you scared the shit out of me!" I yelled.

"My bad," Remy apologized.

"Why you standing over there in the corner like that?" I asked.

"I just wanted to make sure you were good," he answered walking over.

"Oh. Well yeah I'm okay." I told him.

"Cool."

"Are you okay?" I asked him as he walked by me.

"Yeah. I just didn't like how I came at you earlier. I know you was just making conversation and shit," he confessed. "I don't know. I guess just still thinking about it gets me in a fucked-up place."

"You're good Remy." I told him. "Trust me, I've been in the same space before. When my mom passed, it was like a part of me died. So trust me I understand."

I walked over to him and gave him a hug forgetting the fact that a bitch was just standing there in a towel. Of course, when I raised my arms to hug him, the towel fucking dropped to the floor. I scrambled to pick it up and cover myself while this nigga took a step back and grinned.

"Gah damn," he cheesed. "I see why Dymond ass was jealous."

I covered myself quickly and tried to hide my embarrassment.

"Sorry," I flushed.

"Don't be," he said pulling me back to him. "Cause what I saw ain't nothing to be embarrassed about."

I opened my mouth to talk and he covered it with his. I felt his hands scoop my ass and before I knew it he picked me up and my legs were wrapped around his waist.

I knew my ass should've gone home.

REMY

"Mmm…oh shit. Shit! R—R—Remy!"

"*Damn this pussy feels good.*" I grunted digging deeper into Skyy's pussy.

"*Oh God! Remy I'm cummin!*"

I could feel her pussy grip me as she exploded and screamed in my ear.

"*Ah shit!*" she cried out.

I covered her lips with mine kissing her hard and deep, rapidly exploring her mouth with my tongue. She matched me and ravaged me with hers. Her moans were driving me fucking crazy and I wanted to bust all in her pussy. I had to control this shit.

I pulled out to keep from cummin and made my way down to her pussy. I noticed how neat it was. She had a bikini wax and it had a little hair on it. I spread them lips wide and dove in, my tongue making patterns as she hissed and squirmed.

"*Mmm.*" I mumbled tasting her.

I felt her hands on the back of my head and held her shaking legs.

"*Oh God! Oh fuck! Remy!*" she screamed.

She tried to run but I grabbed her by her waist and held her down tight. The more I licked, the harder she came and bucked while still trying to get away.

"Stop fighting." I said in between sucking her pearl and catching all her juices.

Damn this girl was amazing.

"Remy stop! I can't take no more!" she cried.

I sat up and looked at her smirking as she tried to catch her breath.

"You really want me stop?" I asked.

She opened her mouth but nothing came out.

"I didn't think so." I said pushing her back down and getting back to my meal.

"I knew you were gonna be amazing." I told her playing with her pussy.

She cried out feeling my tongue spinning in circles and putting two of my fingers in her shit. The combination and how fast I was going was fucking her all the way up. Just when she was about to nut again, I stopped and put my dick back in feeling her gush all over my shit. I put my fingers in her mouth so she could taste what I did.

I stroked her slow and deep and while she grinded on me, I placed one of her perfectly round and supple nipples in my mouth sucking and biting and making her dig her nails in my back. I took them sexy legs of hers and pushed them back over her head making her scream feeling me get all the way in her shit.

"Gah damn." I huffed feeling how her pussy was flowing.

A nigga was about to bust. Her shit was so tight and wet. Her walls were damn near contracting around my dick. I was getting lost in her. Skyy had that kind of pussy that a nigga would intentionally get a chic pregnant over.

Bzzz. Bzzz. Bzzz.

I opened my eyes to hear my phone buzzing.

"Shit." I mumbled, fully opening my eyes and seeing the bright ass sun beaming in through my living room windows.

I was dreaming about how I had sexed Skyy literally a few hours ago. I wasn't expecting it to go down but a nigga wasn't mad that it did either. The shit was epic. Seeing her in that towel I was already fighting pushing her ass against that wall and fucking her up to the ceiling. But when that shit dropped and I saw her body, I couldn't help myself. I had to have her. I damn near tore my clothes trying to get it off so fast. Her shit was tight and I didn't want to leave that bed.

We fucked for hours but when we were done, she did some weird shit and turned her back to me and asked me to leave. I thought she would want me there but she curved my ass. I ain't going to lie, it fucked my head up for a minute. But fuck it. I gave her what she wanted and took my ass back to the couch. Still, I wanted to explore her more and have some more fun with her before she left.

Bzzz. Bzzz. Bzzz.

"What the fuck."

I picked up my phone off the floor to answer it.

"Hello." I said.

"Well it's about time you answered your phone! I've been calling you all night!" Dymond screamed into the phone.

I wasn't trying to hear her bullshit this early in the damn morning. I looked at my phone and saw that it was 10:23 am. Why the fuck was she calling me so fucking early? I had just went to sleep like an hour and a half ago.

"Do you hear me talking to you? Hello?" she screeched. "Do you not know I've been calling you all night?"

"Yeah I know. I'm looking at the fucking seventeen missed calls and text messages." I told her scrolling through my phone.

"What the fuck is wrong with you?"

"Ain't nothing wrong with me. What the fuck is wrong with you calling me on some bullshit?" I shot back.

"Because! You wanna sit up here and try to play me out at the club in front of everybody like I'm some bird on the street. Like you ain't been up in my shit fucking me!" she whined. "I'm sick of this shit with you Rem!"

"Then why the fuck are you on my goddamn phone right now?" I sighed. I rubbed my forehead trying to figure out just how dumb this girl was. "Aye yo you gotta be a special kind of stupid to still be chasing a nigga. Bruh, I told you in front of fuckin everybody that I don't want your ass. Besides…my dick ain't all that remember?"

Her ass got quiet and I could tell she knew she fucked up.

"You know I only said that because I was mad at how you were all up in that bitch face," she tried to explain. "You got me in there looking stupid."

"No yo dumb ass got you in there looking stupid." I argued. "I ain't got time to be dealing with your psychotic ass."

"Oh, but you got time for her?" She snapped.

"Yo are you really fucking slow?" I asked. This bitch was a new kind of stupid. "We fucking done. I told your ass last night exactly what the fuck it was. So what the fuck you calling me for? What the fuck do you want."

"I want you!" She screeched sounding like she was crying.

"Oh my God!" I groaned. "Yo, don't start this bullshit. Cause them tears ain't fazing me."

"Really Remy?" She sniffed. "All this time we been fucking with each other and you just gone do some shit like that?"

"Dymond don't come at me with that dramatic shit." I said. "Real shit, you already know what the fuck it was. I told you I ain't tryna be with your ass like that. We were just fucking. We ain't date. We ain't kick it like that. You hooked me up with a connect at the club to run some work through. But other than that, me and you wasn't on no chill type vibe. I told you from jump, I ain't tryna have no girl. You said you could handle the shit so don't be coming to me acting like I broke your goddamn heart. Cut the Young & the Restless soap opera shit. This ain't no damn romance novel. We fucked. The pussy was good. That's it."

"So me hooking you up, you breaking me off with money and shit, and you always coming by the club?" she interrupted. "What was all of that?"

"That's fucking business yo!" I stressed. "I hooked you up with bread because you gave me the spot at the club. That ain't on no rela-tionship type shit. Why the fuck would I be with a stripper? Why would I want other niggas looking at my girl and shit like that? And I know I ain't the only nigga sliding up in there right now. Only reason you coming at me is cause your ass jealous of ole girl."

"Ain't nobody jealous of her uglass," she spat.

"Yea aight." I snorted. "I still ain't fucking with you like that so, I don't know why your stupid ass ain't getting the shit."

"You know what Remy? Fuck you!" she started crying. "I don't need you. I'm done."

"Cool." I said hanging up the phone before she could say another word.

Why the fuck this chic was calling me in the first goddamn place I don't know. It was something seriously wrong with that broad. I know dick makes people do crazy shit but damn! Her ass was just stupid. I was tired of dealing with the shit. The bullshit she pulled with Skyy fucked me up. That let me know she had folks up in that club thinking I was her nigga and shit. This wasn't no Bonnie & Clyde type shit. I made a lot of money out that club.

My mind drifted back to Skyy and how she didn't even want to talk to my ass after what happened between us. Normally I would've just left the shit alone but she seemed cool. She wasn't sweating me like Dymond was. Shit, my ass was laid up on the couch while she was sleeping in my room. I could tell that she was different. She didn't need to be in that damn club. It would eat her alive. She was way too naïve for that shit.

Damn why am I even worried about her like that? Shit. I done told her about Nikki and everything. I didn't know why that shit bugged me but it did. Nobody knew about that shit. Why I told her I didn't know. Shit, I did. I was feeling her. But I couldn't. I ain't even know her like that.

"Good morning." I heard.

I looked up and saw her standing there in her t-shirt watching me.

"Oh hey what's up?" I spoke.

"Um...I was just wondering if maybe I could get a ride back home?" she asked.

"Yea I got you." I yawned.

I sat up off the couch and grabbed the shorts that I had sitting at the other end. I looked at her and noticed how the t-shirt barely covered her ass. My eyes started roaming up and down her body remembering how it felt in between them thighs.

"You okay?" she asked as I stood up.

"Yea I'm straight." I nodded putting my shorts on.

I peeped her looking at me while I got dressed. She could keep looking for all I cared. Shit I wanted to bend her over one more time.

I stopped when I heard her mumble something.

"What you say?" I asked.

"I didn't say anything," she shook her head.

The way that she was looking though I could tell she was lying.

"Aight let me go brush my teeth real quick." I told her.

She nodded and stood there like she wanted to say something but changed her mind and went back in the bedroom. I took a few minutes to get myself together and came back in the living room to find her sitting on the couch playing on her phone.

"Are you ready?" I asked noticing she wasn't looking at me.

"Yeah," she nodded still in her phone.

"Aight let's roll."

We hopped in the car and I pulled up her homegirls address on my phone. She was quiet pretty much the entire drive.

"Yo, you sure you good?" I asked.

"Yup," she nodded. "I'm just a little tired. Tierra done called me a few times so I know she's probably worried."

"Well, tell her she doesn't have to worry." I smiled. "You're in good hands."

"Yeah and them good hands clearly got me into more trouble," she said side eyeing me.

I knew she was gone say some shit. Now I was going to have to hear how I took advantage of her or I shouldn't have done it or some shit.

"Yo, my bad." I said hoping she wouldn't start tripping. "A nigga just couldn't help himself. I tripped out."

"No," she shook her head. "It's not all your fault. I knew you and Dymond had a situation."

"Nah." I shut her down quick turning the corner. "I told you. I don't do relationship drama. I got other shit to worry about than a female. I ain't with that girl."

"Well...you may not be with *that girl* but she's damn sure with you," she argued.

"And she knows what's up." I corrected her. "Ain't no confusion. She already know I ain't fuckin with her like that."

"Well, truthfully, it's a little more than that," she admitted.

I glanced at her while I switched lanes and saw she was fidgeting a little.

Here we go.

"What's up?" I asked as if I didn't already know.

"Remy, I just...I didn't mean to come off so strong like that," she apologized. "I know it sounds fucked up but...I just wanted to do something that I knew would piss my ex off. I wanted to see what it was like to fuck around on him like he did me."

Damn. Shawty was cold blooded. I didn't even know what to say on that shit. I thought she would have been on some bullshit and trying to claim me but she shocked the hell out of me with that.

"Well if he was getting any of what I got, I don't see how that nigga could be fucking around." I complimented her. "That was like the pot of gold at the end of a rainbow kinda good."

She blushed and I smiled.

"But you good." I dismissed. "Just glad I could be of service."

She smirked and I took the exit the GPS instructed me to take.

"So you working tonight?" I asked looking down at my phone to see my mama calling me.

I was going to have to call her back when I dropped Skyy off. I knew she was probably going to ask if I had been by to see Nikki's mama.

"Yeah," she nodded.

"You need me to come and get you?"

She snapped her head and looked at me like I had lost my damn mind.

"Are you crazy?" she shrieked.

"What?" I asked confused. "I was just saying I could come scoop you if you needed me to."

"Why?" she pressed frowning and getting worked up. "Like do you just want me to fight this bitch or something?"

"She ain't gone do shit." I told her. "But my bad."

"Yeah uh huh," she said. "Just like you said that you not about the drama, neither am I."

"I feel you." I said taking the next turn. "I was trying to help you out. I know you ain't got a whip right now."

"I can always get my homegirl to take me," she shrugged yawning. "And Uber isn't that bad. Besides...I'm not trying to be funny, you seem like a cool nigga and all and I appreciate everything that you've done for me, but—"

"Oh shit am I getting friend zoned? Is this what it feels like?" I joked laughing.

She looked at me and I winked making her relax. She smiled and shook her head.

"I know you probably have females just throwing themselves at you and all of that, but I'm not one of those," she told me.

"Didn't say you were baby girl." I said. "But, I would catch you quick."

I smiled seeing her eyes get big and she ducked her head. She was cute.

"I ain't gon lie. I do kinda wanna see what's up with you." I admitted.

"Um...that's cool but, I'm just trying to make my money so that I can do what I need to do," she said shutting me down.

"And what's that?" I asked her.

"Get me an apartment. And be on my own," she said simply.

"Damn. So you done with ole boy for real huh?"

"Pretty much," she nodded.

"Damn. Okay I hear you." I was kind of impressed. She seemed like she had an agenda. But shit, so did a lot of girls at the strip club. Then they got sucked in. Something was telling me that Skyy would prove me wrong though. "Well like I said, I don't have a problem picking you up."

She shook her head ignoring me and I turned onto her street. I pulled up to her friends house and parked the car.

"So I'll pick you up at like what nine?" I asked.

She looked at me and sighed.

"You're relentless aren't you?"

"You can say that." I smiled at her again.

She shook her head and I could see her hesitation.

"Remy—"

"Damn girl I'm just taking you to work! It ain't like I'm asking you to marry me or no shit like that. Yo, I'm just being nice. And you got relationship drama." I smirked.

Her mouth dropped open and I bust out laughing. She realized I was clowning and started laughing too.

"You know what? I can't with you." She grabbed her stuff and gave in. "Fine. You can pick me up."

"Aight cool." I smiled sarcastically. "Now I can have a good day."

"Yeah well, you have your good day. I'm bout to go back to sleep," she yawned.

She hopped out and I watched her walk to the door. She didn't even look to see if I was waiting on her. She just walked in the house and closed the door.

She was just like me but with a pussy. Damn. This shit was about to be interesting.

SKYY

"Umm…bitch you want to tell me where the fuck you were all night?"

"Well good morning to you too!" I yawned sitting up in the bed.

"Girl it ain't morning. It's fucking two o'clock in the damn afternoon!"

"You lying!" I said picking up my phone and looking at the time.

I wiped my eyes and saw that she was right. Damn. I had been knocked the hell out. Remy had brought me back to the house a few hours ago but considering that we had stayed up all night, I didn't get much sleep so as soon as my head hit the pillow, I was out.

"So back to my question." Tierra said. "Where the hell were you? You had me nervous as hell. I almost called Malachi's ass."

"Oooh girl don't do that." I said. "But no I'm good. I was at work last night and then I met somebody."

"You met somebody? At the strip club? Aight Ebony," she joked trying to call me the bitch from the movie The Players Club.

"Aht aht. Don't do it." I said. "It wasn't nothing like that. I wasn't fucking no niggas for money. This dumb ass girl from the club got real stupid cause of him."

"What you mean?" she asked walking over and sitting on the edge of the bed.

I told her everything that happened with Dymond and how she had destroyed my stuff after I gave Remy a lap dance.

"Oh hell no!" She said. "You shoulda drug that hoe."

"Oh trust I wanted to." I told her. "I really wanted to, but you know I gotta make this money. And Remy embarrassed the fuck out of this girl T. It was hilarious."

"Bitches kill me tryna come at the next chic cause they nigga don't wanna deal with they raggedy asses no more," she fussed. "Is he fine?"

I shook my head and laughed.

"Really Tierra?"

"What?" she shrugged. "I mean...well bitch he got to be fine for you to be gone all night. Was the dick good?"

"Why am I friends with you?" I laughed falling back on the pillow.

"Wait let me smell your breath," she went on. "You got dick breath?"

"Bitch get out!" I laughed throwing a pillow at her and hitting her on the side of the head.

"You fucked him didn't you?" she said eyeballing me.

I tried to avoid her stare but it was obvious.

"Oh my God! I knew it!" she squealed. "No wonder that bitch came after you. Okay so what happened? Tell me everything."

"Honestly, the shit just happened." I told her. "Like I can't say I necessarily planned it."

"So you just happened to land on his dick?" she laughed.

"No." I huffed. "Dymond pulled that dumb shit and I was ready to dip. He offered to take me to get some more clothes since I was walking around damn near naked and then we went to get something to eat at IHOP. By the time we left it was late and your ass was knocked out of course. So we went back to his crib."

"Mmhmm. And you bust it open for a real nigga," she teased.

"I—swear—to—God—I—can't—stand—you." I clapped. "No that is not how it went down. That's just you."

"Bitch fuck you!" she laughed laying down.

"No we were talking about stuff that was kind of...personal and I gotta admit, I didn't think the nigga was that deep." I told her. "But you know we started talking and I guess feelings just happened and shit. I went to take a shower and then next thing I know bitch that nigga had my soul floating around the damn room."

"Damn!" she said.

"I know." I smiled recalling how good it was. "Like that nigga fucked the shit out of me."

"Better than Malachi?" she asked.

I nodded quickly.

"Oh hell yea." I giggled. "Baby that thang had a curve to it. And his tongue game? Shat!"

"Get it bitch!" she squealed high fiving me. "Well just be careful. Because you know that you still got Malachi's ass lurking around."

"Fuck Malachi." I snapped. My phone rang and of course it was his ass calling. "Speak of the damn devil." I swiped ignoring his call.

I didn't have anything to say to him. I was so tired of him dictating every single thing that I did. My phone buzzed again notifying me that Malachi had sent a text this time.

"What?" Tierra asked frowning.

"Nothing." I told her. "Malachi ass just being his usual asshole self. Telling me that I need to stop ignoring him and we need to talk about this like adults. I ain't got shit to say to him."

My phone vibrated again but I relaxed when I saw that it was Remy.

Remy: I'll be there at 9 on the dot. Be ready.

I sent him a quick reply letting him know that I was awake and would be ready.

"Well, if you need to go get some more outfits I'm going to the mall in a bit." Tierra said.

"Cool." I said getting up out of bed. "Let me go wash my ass."

"Yeah cause you smell like a stripper that made some bad decisions and some sweaty dick right now," she joked.

I flipped her the finger and got up to head to the bathroom.

After about forty-five minutes and a good hot shower, we were out the house ready to hit the stores. I didn't want to spend too much money but I didn't really have a lot of options.

"So what is this Remy dude like?" Tierra asked as we walked through the mall.

"He's cool." I told her. "Single. Twenty-six. Chocolate. Buff. Tattoos everywhere. Typical dope boy."

"No kids that you know of?" she pressed.

I shook my head at my goofy ass friend.

"Damn T, not every nigga gotta be a baby daddy." I said. "But no he doesn't have any kids. And aside from him having questionable taste in women, he seems to be pretty chill."

"Mmhmm," she nodded walking into Rainbow. "He got any cute friends?"

"I mean, I wasn't really paying attention to them like that, but he got a few homies." I told her. "I think one of them got a girl though. But I'm sure you might like one of them with your little hot ass."

My phone rang interrupting our conversation and once again it was Malachi.

"What?" I snapped answering the phone.

"Is that how you answer your phone?" he said.

I hung up and saw a few people in the store looking in our direction.

"I'm going outside real quick." I told her knowing his stupid ass was about to call right back.

Sure enough my phone buzzed in my hand.

"What do you want?"

"Skyy is this really how you want to handle this?" he spoke. "Why are you ignoring me?"

"Malachi I told you I'm not doing this no more." I explained trying to keep my voice down. "I'm tired of you trying to dictate everything I do and every move that I make. Newsflash. I am a grown ass woman. Not some kid in elementary school."

"Skyy...please. Just listen to me," he pleaded. "I didn't mean to act like that. You know that I'm a patient man. I was just at my wits end. It was late, I was exhausted, and you were out all night—"

"Are you serious right now?" I shrieked. "You still tryna put the blame on me?"

"No! Skyy, I'm just—I'm not trying to argue with you. Look I'm sorry," he apologized.

"You're always sorry." I pointed out. "Every time I turn around you're apologizing. You let me leave the other night and didn't even try to stop me. You didn't call to see if I was okay. You took my name off the accounts? Does that sound like somebody who's sorry?"

"I know," he admitted. "I figured you just needed to cool off."

"By letting me walk out in the middle of the night with all of my shit?" I pushed. "Do you know I almost got jacked?"

"Huh?"

"I almost got robbed!" I rolled my eyes forgetting I was talking to his bougie ass.

"What?" He said surprised. "Why didn't you say anything?"

"Oh don't try to act like you care now." I told him. "Because you didn't then. If you did, you wouldn't have put your girlfriend out at two in the morning!"

"Skyy I didn't put you out. You left," he argued.

"Yea after you packed my shit." I reminded him.

"Skyy, please. Just come home. Are you coming home?"

"No!" I hissed. I had to calm down because I could feel myself getting heated and I was drawing too much attention. I took a deep breath and continued to try and talk to him. "Look Malachi, I cared about you and I loved you okay? And I appreciate you for the good times that we did have, but I can't do it anymore. Like I got other things that I wanna do."

"Like what? Hair?" he fired back. "Party with your friend that's encouraging you to end a five year relationship?"

I sucked my teeth and shook my head.

"See? That's exactly what I'm talking about. Look at how you're talking to me." I told him. "You're making it seem like what I want is just some bullshit."

"Because I know that you can do something better honey," he fussed. "So you're mad at me because I want you to do better?"

"Better to whose standards though? Yours?" I questioned. "At the end of the day no matter what I wanna do all you should worry about is being supportive. But no, you try to make it seem like I'm just making a mistake or something."

"Because you—"

"Don't." I said interrupting him. "The only mistake I made was answering this phone. Goodbye."

I hung up not giving him a chance to respond and Tierra walked out and looked at me concerned.

"You okay?" she asked.

"Yeah." I nodded. "Trust me, I'm straight."

"What he say?" she asked.

"Just the usual dumb shit. Trying to make it seem like he didn't do anything wrong." I explained. "I cant stand his anal retentive ass.

"Girl, I been telling you Malachi's ass is so fucking extra," she shook her head. "I bet that he gives instructions during sex," she joked making me laugh.

It worked because I burst out laughing.

"You so goddamn dumb!"

"I'm serious!" she urged. "I bet his dick came with a manual didn't it?

"Yo, I swear to God there are some screws loose in your head." I said. "Like I really wonder how we became friends."

"Because you know I keep it real and tell the truth and I make your crazy ass smile," she reminded me.

"True." I nodded still laughing.

"But on some real shit, do you really want to just be done with him?" she asked getting serious.

"I've thought about it and even though shit's been crazy, I know I can't go back to him." I explained. "I just can't. I haven't felt more relaxed than I had in the last couple of days."

"Well bitch you know you can stay with me for as long as you want," she offered.

"I appreciate it." I said hugging my friend.

She was literally all I had and I really was grateful for her.

I texted Remy seeing that I had a message from him while I was on the phone. He had texted me a few times since I had been out with Tierra. I hated that I fucked him already. But, I was curious. But knowing that he had all that drama with Dymond worried me. And he was slanging through the club. He never outright said anything to me about it but, I wasn't stupid. What other reason would he have to be in there if he wasn't fucking with none of the girls.

Remy was fine as hell. I remembered feeling his body pressed against mine and looking at all those tattoos. His skin was soft and smooth and he smelled like Ocean by Bath and Body Works. I remembered licking his chest and feeling him push that massive dick in my pussy. I hadn't been fucked like that ever. It was wild. It was erotic. It was crazy and nasty. It was pleasurable.

We spent a few hours shopping, grabbing something to eat, and at the last minute decided to get our nails done. By the time we got back to the house, it was almost eight o'clock and Remy was picking me up soon. He was doing me a favor taking me to work so I wanted to make sure that I was on time like he said.

I don't know how he got anything done that day because we spent the whole day texting each other. He was hilarious to say the least and he definitely kept a smile on my face. I was actually looking forward to seeing him. I learned a lot about him the night before and even though I wasn't trying to get with him other than that one time smash, he was somebody that held my interest.

At nine on the dot, Remy was there to pick me up so I grabbed my overnight bag with my new outfits and headed outside to hop in his truck. He gave me a quick smile and I became all giddy and happy inside but played it cool.

"You bout to go to the gym or something?" He laughed looking at my appearance.

I was in some sweats that I had bought from Rainbow.

"I don't need to be in there all dressed up." I told him.

"I feel you," he nodded. "You ain't wearing that crazy ass wig are you?"

"No." I laughed. "I got a new one."

"Why you don't just wear your hair?" he asked looking at my natural shoulder length hair.

"Because I don't want it smelling like smoke." I told him.

"Makes sense," he said. "So what you been up to all day?"

"As if you didn't know." I laughed. "Talking to your crazy ass on the phone. And I went shopping with Tierra. That's how I got some new stuff." I said holding my bag up.

"That's wassup," he said merging onto the highway.

"What about you?"

"I talked to your ass and chilled a little bit," he told me.

I peeped his gear while he drove. He was dressed in all black and had a basic gold chain on. His arms was all oiled up and shit and the way his ass was looking I wanted to hop on his dick right now. He was talking about something but I couldn't focus because I was too busy looking.

He caught my stare and I quickly looked away. It was quiet for a hot second but Remy started joking and I relaxed. We laughed and joked all the way to the club. I was kind of antsy though the closer that we got there because I knew it was going to be some bullshit. I just hoped that Dymond's ass wasn't there. Maybe then I could just work and relax. But of course, luck was not on my side because the minute that Remy pulled up, some girl saw him and ran inside. Before I could even get out of the truck, Dymond was standing at the door just staring at me like I was Rent-A-Center coming to get her damn furniture.

"Here we go." I sighed as we hopped out.

"Nah, don't even worry about it," he insisted. "She ain't gone do shit. Not while I'm here."

"Oh so you staying all night?" I asked side eyeing him.

He grabbed my bag and walked in with me.

"Yep. Otherwise who else gone take you home?" he smiled.

"Damn, can you say that shit a little bit louder so she can hear you." I gritted trying not to have folks paying attention to us.

"Shit I don't give a fuck," he scoffed. "Let they asses know. I came here for you not her."

"Mmhmm. You sure you ain't fuck with nobody other than Dymond?" I asked looking around and seeing how practically all eyes were on us.

"Man hell nah," he said. "I handle business. And Dymond know that. That's why I said don't trip. She know shit can go left for her real quick."

"Mmk." I said as I took my bag off of him and walked away from the bar heading to the dressing room.

The way Dymond's ass was glaring at me and how scared all these other broads was acting, I believed him. There was no way in hell another bitch would even try. She acted like she was his girl.

She looked at me and rolled her eyes but kept her mouth shut and got up. I thought she was ready to square up and I was damn sure ready to fade that ass up but she just stomped past me out the room to the floor.

I don't know what the fuck happened but, I didn't have time for it. They could have this shit. I was just trying to get this money and get the fuck out.

REMY

"You know I'm trying to be cool about this, but yo girl got one more time to eyeball me or mumble some slick shit under her breath and I promise you that bitch can catch a fade." Skyy snapped walking up to me.

"What the fuck happened now?"

"Her ass being fucking extra and shit. Like I ain't got time for the shit."

"Yo, what is it with y'all females man?" I asked no one in particular.

I didn't understand how broads could hold a grudge for so long. Shit, it had been two fucking weeks since Skyy started working at that damn club and Dymond was still on that bull shit. I knew she wasn't going to do shit though because if she did, she wouldn't get her percentage of the work that came through there. Half them hoes in there was either bringing in customers for me or on it they damn selves. Not to mention I had the owners pockets lined up.

"Every day that I'm in there, she acting like she wanna do something." Skyy ranted. "She got all these bitches in there talking shit and tryna take customers and shit. I try to get a dance or some shit, and here she come flashing her titties and ass all in they face. Then my music got fucked up. Oh and my phone came up missing and I got locked out. Her ass tried to get in my shit! I'm just trying to make my damn money so I can get the fuck out of here. But no, this bitch wanna keep testing me. She keep testing me and she gone pass."

Skyy was pissed off. She had been trying to make money that night and every time she turned around some shit was happening. Now the shit was starting to get on my nerves because it was fucking with my business. Seeing Skyy so riled up had a nigga wanting to fuck that stress out of her. Shit she looked bad as hell when she was mad. But she was mad so I was trying to block that shit out.

I grabbed her shit and walked up to the front so we could leave. Skyy had barely made payout so she was ready to go.

"Yo, why don't you go wait in the truck?" I told her. "I need to handle some shit in here real quick."

"Yea," she mumbled taking my keys and walking out to the truck.

I headed to the bar and talked to Shawn real quick. He gave me the money for the night and I peeped Dymonds ass staring at me from the entrance of the dressing room.

"Yo I need to holla at Dymond ass real quick." I told him.

"Go head," he nodded as I slid him a quarter brick.

I walked to the dressing room and Dymond went back in when she saw me coming.

"Nah don't run off now." I said walking in the room. I headed straight to her and grabbed her by her arm pushing her against the old dusty wall. "Listen to me and listen to me good. Cut the bullshit and cut it now!"

"What the fuck are you talking about?" she growled trying to break free of my grasp. "You're hurting me. Let go."

"I'ma do a lot worse if you keep this shit up." I warned.

"I ain't done shit to you or your little bitch," she sneered.

"Bullshit." I gritted. I got so close up on her our noses were touching. "Dymond don't bite the fucking hand that feeds you. Now I'm warning you. All the little stunts you pulled tonight? That ends. Ain't no more talking shit. No more taking her customers and shit and fucking up her music. Dead it or I'm gone remind you of what the fuck happens when you cross me."

She was standing there teary-eyed, but she didn't say shit. She knew her limits and she knew that I meant everything I said.

"Glad we got an understanding." I told her. "You do what the fuck I tell you and get my money."

I let her go and she snatched away all dramatic. I backed up and turned around seeing everybody else watching.

"And that goes for the rest of you bitches too." I announced. "Y'all know wassup."

The room was so quiet you could hear a rat piss on cotton. I walked out leaving her standing there looking shook and headed to the truck. Skyy was sitting in the passenger seat still seething. I hopped in and closed the door. It was a little cool outside and she had taken my sweatshirt and pretty much made it hers.

"You good?" I said putting the car in drive.

"Yea," she answered bland.

She wasn't even looking at me. Her eyes stayed trained out the window.

"Look don't trip on Dymond ass." I told her. "That shit is handled. She just hating and shit."

"But for what though?" she shrieked turning to me. "Because of you? I didn't chase you. I didn't come after you. Hell, I just come in there, work and go home. That's it."

She was riled up but I couldn't blame her. She was close to making the money that she needed to make. I had taken her to work every night for the last couple of weeks but she cut back to working just weekends because of the bullshit that was happening. She only had a few more weekends to work and she would be good. She had been applying for jobs and everything and had a few leads. When her homegirl was at work, I was taking her around so she could look for apartments and all that. Shit was cool.

"I'll be glad when I make this money and can get the hell out of that damn club for good," she said.

Secretly, I was thinking the same thing. Shorty didn't really need to be in there. The shit wasn't for her. Plus, whenever I was in there, the way them niggas was tryna get at her low key had me irked. I knew she wasn't the type to get down like that but I wasn't feeling the shit. I didn't want nobody else looking at what I had.

"Hello? Did you hear me?" she said interrupting my thoughts.

"My bad wassup? What you say?" I asked.

"I said where we going to eat?" she asked.

"Oh. Aight. Let's go to Cook Out." I suggested.

"Cool," she agreed. "I could go for a chicken sandwich tray with double fries and a banana pudding shake right now."

I headed to the Cook Out by the house and looked over to see her still frowned up.

"Yo, don't sweat that Dymond shit." I told her again. "She on some bullshit right now cause she see I'm giving you the attention her ass ain't get. She'll meet another nigga and be straight."

"Yea well she need to hurry up and meet another nigga cause I'm telling you I'm with the shits," she spat. "I ain't the one for the games. I'll beat that hoes ass."

I looked over at her and smirked.

"Look at Little Miss Suburbs trying to fight somebody." I joked.

"Suburbs my ass. Don't let that shit fool you. I'm from the streets," she said. "I'm from the tre four. It ain't nothing for me to drag a hoe."

"I hear you." I said trying not to laugh.

This shit was funny. My phone rang and Dymond's name popped up on the display screen in the car. Skyy started frowning seeing her name. She hit the answer icon before I could stop her.

"He's with his girl bitch so stop calling with your thirsty ass!" she yelled before hanging up.

I was glad we were pulling into the drive thru of the Cook Out because a nigga was hollering ready to fall out the truck laughing.

"Yoooo…" I said in disbelief. "You wildin!"

"Why the fuck is she still calling you?" she asked. "Like the bitch got me all the way fucked up."

I pulled around behind the other cars still laughing and eventually she started laughing too.

"My bad," she apologized. "I'm just tired of her ass."

"You good." I told her creeping through the line. "So you wanna be my girl and shit huh?"

"Boy hush," she dismissed. "I just said that shit to irritate her."

"Yea okay. You know you want me."

"No. I know you want me," she said turning to me. Her eyes questioning me.

"Hell yea I want your ass!" I said. "Shit, why else would I be taking your ass to work every night and doing all of this other sucka shit?"

Her mouth dropped open and I let out another laugh.

"Well damn. I thought you were doing it just because you were being nice," she said.

"I am." I said as I pulled up to the speaker box of the order menu and placed our order.

After we grabbed our food, we headed back to my spot. She was going to crash on my couch since her homegirl had some nigga at the crib. We drove in silence and I thought about her calling herself my girl to Dymond. I know she was just saying that shit to piss her off, but the shit sounded good.

"Yo, keep it a buck. You wouldn't give a nigga like me a chance for real?" I asked.

"Right now?" she said slowly chewing her food. "I don't know. I mean, you know I've only been with one other nigga and then me and you kind of did our thing hella fast. It's only been maybe two months since I broke up with Malachi," she explained. "I'm not really in the position to be thinking about a relationship. That was the whole point of me breaking up with Malachi. I want to get a regular job and just focus on me. Get my own place. Get my own car. Not have to depend on nobody else."

"I feel you." I nodded.

I could respect that. She had goals which was more than I could say about most of them bitches in that club. But shit, it made her more desirable.

"Besides…you got a stalker my nigga," she teased.

"Oh you got jokes."

My phone vibrated and she started laughing.

"See?"

I looked and saw it was Dre.

"Waddup?" I answered.

Dre started rambling and I listened for a few minutes before I hung up.

"Everything okay?" she asked.

"Yea. Dre talking bout he's at his old lady spot and she flipping out on his ass and he need me to scoop him up because she hid his keys." I told her. "He want me to take him to his baby mama house."

"Well, now I see why she trippin," she said. "Especially if he tryna go straight to his baby mama's."

"Yea well... I'ma drop you at the crib and then go scoop him." I informed her.

"Okay. That's fine," she shrugged.

I drove the rest of the way to the crib dropping her off. She grabbed the rest of her food and went in. I was ready to hurry up and go get this nigga. I knew she would probably be asleep when I got back but I wanted her. And I was going to make her mine.

I scooped Dre's ass up looking crazy. His girl was going off standing on the porch cussing that nigga straight out. They asses looked crazy at three in the damn morning going off on each other. He got in the car and she nodded grabbing something big off the porch and walking over to his car. I watched her swing and hit the nigga's windshield.

"Yo what the fuck is wrong with you!" Dre yelled hopping out the truck and running over to his car.

He had a C-class that was parked in her driveway and she was going ham on that bitch. She started swinging at him with it and he backed up calling her all kinds of crazy and shit. I didn't have these problems. This was some hood shit.

Eventually he got back in the truck and I listened to him rant about how his girl had gone through his phone and seen texts between him and some other bitch. She started fucking his shit up and he went off. Now his car was fucked up and was probably going to be a lot worse the next day when he came back to get it.

I didn't even know what the fuck to say so I just dropped that nigga at his baby mama's. Next time that nigga was going to have to catch an Uber.

I headed back to the crib exhausted. I found my mind wandering to Skyy. I wondered if she would ever do some shit like that to me. She didn't strike me as the type but everybody has a breaking point. She had been chilling with all this shit going on with Dymond so I didn't think she would pop off like that. Plus she never mentioned doing any crazy shit to her ex.

Skyy had done something that no female since Nikki had done and I didn't even realize it. She had got into my head. I enjoyed picking her up and taking her to the club. Even when I was making money and handling business, she would drift into my thoughts. Shit was easy with her. When we would hang out, it was like being with one of the bruhs but, she was just cute. She didn't trip out when females were around. She wasn't sweating me. She was just chill.

I pulled up to the crib and headed up the stairs to my apartment. When I walked in, I could hear the TV. I walked to the bedroom and saw her sleeping. I walked in and took the food off the bed, putting it on the nightstand beside her.

Looking down at her, she was gorgeous. She didn't really need to do a bunch of make-up and her hair was wrapped up. Her lips were plump and begging for me to suck them. She had a tank top on and her titty was threatening to fall out and expose itself to me. I could feel myself getting hard. We hadn't done anything since that first night but I wanted to explore all of her again.

She stirred in her sleep and I left out going to hop in the shower. I handled my shit and got out, drying off. I had to grab a shirt out of my dresser and when I walked back into the room, she had moved to where her ass was peeking out from the covers. I couldn't take this shit.

I bent down and kissed her skin, grabbing her ass and massaging it while I started kissing her on her thighs. She moaned and I turned her on her back, my dick getting hard as I made my way in between her thighs. I was craving her pussy.

I started to lick and kiss the inside of her thighs moving her panties to the side so I could get to her moist lips. She moaned once more before opening her eyes and connecting her gaze to mine.

"What are you doing?" she whispered.

"Skyy I want you." I told her taking my tongue and licking her slow from the top of her opening, stopping to suck on her pearl.

She arched her back and I heard her gasp.

"R—R—Remy!" she stuttered. "I can't—I don't—I mean…"

She was trying to talk but I was making it hard for her with the way that I was eating her out. She tasted like heaven if there was such a thing.

"Remy wait," she finally said after struggling.

I stopped and looked at her trying to hide my frustration.

"I ain't him." I told her. "And I ain't never felt nobody like I have you since Nikki."

Her eyes softened and she looked at me with those eyes of hers. She knew I was being sincere with what I was saying.

"Remy," she whispered. "I do like you. But I just don't wanna get played. I mean, what happened before—"

I sat up and covered her lips with mine and we both got lost in each others kiss.

"It's already happening." I told her looking her in the eyes. "Just go with it. I got you. I want you. And I know you want me."

She opened her mouth to object and I slid my fingers in her pussy, going in circles. Her eyes fluttered and she threw her head back.

"Remy. I—"

"Say you want me." I demanded.

"I—I—I—"

I started going faster feeling her wetness as her walls began to contract around my fingers.

"Say it." I repeated.

She moaned and I knew she was close.

"I want you," she finally caved.

I stopped, pulling my fingers out, and covering my body with hers, kissing her and easing myself inside her. She gripped my back and wrapped her legs around me and I began to stroke her slow and deep. She was digging her nails deep into my skin and I knew I was going to feel that shit later. But shit, I didn't care.

I was about to put my name all over her and fuck away any doubt or worry she had. Skyy was mine.

REMY

"You got one more time to switch your little ass past me and I promise you I'ma take you in one of these back rooms and fuck the dog shit out of you."

"Boy if you don't hush and let me finish so we can get the hell out of here."

"I'm just saying. You the one over here trying to get a nigga to fuck somebody up." I said grabbing Skyy's ass.

"Down boy," she smirked. "This is my last night so let me just get it over with."

"Yea aight. I'ma let you make it. For now."

Me and Dre were sitting in the back of the club handling business. It was packed like shit so Dre was making sure that work was moving quick and collecting. I was really there keeping an eye on Skyy and making sure these niggas wasn't getting stupid. Thank God it was her last night at the club because I didn't want my girl in this shit.

She had been pounding the pavement and looking for some legit work these last couple of weeks. She finally found a job at a dental office as an input receptionist making good money. She had saved up enough money to get her own spot and was scheduled to move into her place in a week. I convinced her to stay with me until it was ready.

I didn't mind it at all. Since we had gotten together she was there a lot anyway. She made a nigga want to hurry up and come home. If I wasn't handling business, then I was at home wearing her ass out. We were going out and kicking it and all that but we couldn't keep our hands off each other.

For the first time since my fiancé had died, I was genuinely happy with a chic. Not just any chic but, Skyy. It wasn't no drama. Most of these broads that I smashed were trying to tie me down as soon as they got the dick and shit but shit was just easy with us. It just flowed. Shit was good. Even my mama peeped the difference in me. The way things were going, they would be meeting real soon.

I watched her moving around and smiled. She was looking good and every nigga in there was noticing her.

"Bruh here comes trouble." Dre said.

I looked up to see Dymond making a beeline towards me. I guess one of her little homegirls had told her I was here. She'd been blowing my phone up for the last week every single day. I knew it was probably some bullshit the way she was acting. But I didn't want her. I didn't even say shit to her when I had been in here. After tonight, I wasn't going to see her ass ever again and I was cool with that.

"Hey. I've been calling you every day this week," she said walking up on me.

"I know." I told her. "I saw."

"Damn it Remy why do you always do that?" she whined. "So you saw me calling and just decided not to answer?"

"Pretty much." I said looking past her.

"Wow so that's how we're doing it now?" she huffed.

"Man go on somewhere with yo bobble head ass." Dre dragged.

"Nigga fuck you!" She snapped at him. "Wasn't nobody talking to you."

"And ain't nobody tryna talk to you! So you wasting your time bruh," he laughed.

"Nigga whatever!" she hissed. "You just mad cause I ain't tryna give your dumb ass no fucking pussy."

"Man please. You'll bust it open for anybody with a tip."

I just got up and stood in between the two of them. His ass was drunk and I wasn't trying to be sitting there listening to the two of them go back and forth.

"Dymond what do you want?" I asked tired of the bullshit.

"Look Remy I'm sorry to be running up on you but I really need to talk to you," she repeated. "And you not answering your phone so this was the only option I had."

"What is it?"

She looked around like she was nervous or something.

"Can you come outside please?" She pressed.

"For what? What we gotta talk about? I told you we done."

"Trust me, I do not want you," she said rolling her eyes. "But we need to talk. In private."

Dre was still mumbling something under his breath and had her rolling her eyes. I shook my head at this dumb shit. It was beyond old at this point.

"Man I got shit to do. Besides, Skyy bout to be done." I told her.

"Okay," she snorted. "Ain't nobody tryna interrupt you and your little girlfriend. But either we talk outside or I tell everybody in here including your girl."

"That's supposed to scare me or something?" I said unfazed.

"I don't know," she shrugged. "Does knowing that you got a stripper pregnant scare you?"

I looked at the bitch like she had a third eyeball or something. She was really reaching with this one.

"So you pregnant now?" I snorted.

"You heard me," she said. "So, unless you want me to tell your little girlfriend what's going on, we need to go outside and talk."

She was standing there looking dead ass. Something was telling me she wasn't lying. I looked at my boy who had gotten quiet.

"Man I'll be right back." I told him.

"Handle your business," he said.

"If Skyy comes out, tell her I stepped out real quick." I said.

He nodded and I grabbed Dymond by her arm and pushed her outside.

"Now what the fuck are you talking about you pregnant?" I growled.

"That's why I've been calling your phone all week," she rushed. "If you would have answered your phone and talked to me, then you could've found the shit out differently. But you was being a dick about it."

"Man fuck all that." I dismissed. "C'mon man, you know your ass ain't pregnant."

"Oh word?" she said. I watched her pull something out of her bra top and she slammed it in my hand. "Then what the fuck is this then?"

I unfolded it to see an ultrasound with her name on it.

"Man…"I sucked my teeth. "Why the fuck you got this shit?"

"What the fuck do you mean why I got it?" she said looking at me crazy. "Nigga I just told you I'm pregnant. And before you piss me off and say what I think you're gonna say, it's yours."

"Bullshit." I huffed. "We ain't fucked in like a month. So there's no way that your ass could be pregnant that damn fast."

"No dumbass. I was already pregnant when we had sex the last time," she explained. "I'm ten weeks. Two and a half months. I didn't know because I thought my birth control was working. So all the bullshit about the baby not being yours, you can let that shit go because you know we weren't always using condoms and shit. It's yours."

A nigga was trying to calculate the shit in his head. We had fucked a lot. Most of the time I strapped up but there were a few times that I just pulled out. But shit, Dymond wasn't just fucking with me. I know she wasn't.

She smiled seeing my wheels turning.

"Yea so now that you know, you have time to get ready because in like six and a half months, your ass is gonna be a daddy," she informed me.

"Yo, I don't believe this shit." I sighed.

"That's fine," she shrugged. "You don't have to believe me. But child-support will when that good ole DNA test comes back that it's yours."

"So you not taking care of this shit? You tryna keep this baby?" I asked confused. "For what?"

"Yes Remy!" she huffed. "Just because you dont wanna fuck with me no more don't mean you gotta turn your back on your responsibilities. That is a baby. YOUR BABY. So no, I'm not getting rid of it."

"We ain't even together yo." I reminded her. "You know we was just smashing. So you would really do that and be selfish and keep a baby you know I don't want just to be on some petty shit?"

"Petty?" she asked taking a step back. "How am I being petty cause I don't want to kill my baby?"

"You know I'm with Skyy."

"What the fuck does that gotta do with me?" she yelled. "Like you said, we not together. Cool. But this baby is coming. So your little girlfriend is just gonna have to deal with it."

"Watch your mouth." I warned her.

"I told you, I tried to call you but you wouldn't talk to me," she said.

"Come on Dymond don't be stupid." I shook my head. "You know this shit ain't good. How you expect me to be happy about this shit?"

"I don't," she argued. "But damn Rem. You just come out talking bout I need to have an abortion and shit like I'm not supposed to feel some type of way. Like why put me through this shit?"

"First off you're putting yourself through this. There are other solutions. You don't want to go that route so that's your choice." I told her. "So because you're choosing something else, don't get mad at the kind of conversation that's happening. Nothing I just said should've been taken negatively anyways because it's the truth. I've always kept it a band with you. How you choose to take it is on you. Do I think the baby is mine? Hell no. But I know a nigga wasn't smart so yea it could be mine. I don't think it is but I don't think you need to be having a baby just to try to keep a nigga around."

"So you don't want anything to do with this baby at all?" she asked tearful. "Like at all? You just gonna turn your back on me?"

I sighed running my hand over my head. This shit had me all the way bugged.

"Look, if this kid is mine, I will be a father." I assured her. "The situation isn't ideal and not what I would've hoped for, but I'm not the type of nigga to disown a child that's mine. But that's only after it's been proven that it is mine. So don't expect me to be excited about this."

She actually stood there quiet and looking as if she was ready to break.

"Like I said, when the baby gets here, trust and believe I have no problem going to get a DNA test done because I know what it is," she finally spoke. "You can talk shit about me all you want and call me a hoe and everything but we both know that you were hitting it raw. It was plenty of times where we would fuck and you didn't even bother to put on a condom so don't try to make it seem like it was all my fault. I wasn't in that bed by myself."

Fuck! Why in the hell was this shit happening now?

"Is everything okay?" I heard.

I turned to see Skyy standing at the door looking at both of us.

"Yea everything is straight babe." I told her and cutting my eyes ay Dymond.

"Yup." Dymond nodded. "I was just giving Remy what I owed him."

She started to walk back in the club and passed Skyy who looked like she was ready to knock her on her ass.

"Congrats on y'all relationship," she told her. "See you around Remy."

She walked back inside and Skyy turned back to me.

"What was that?" she asked.

"Nothing." I told her shoving the ultrasound in my back pocket.

"Mmhmm," she nodded.

I could tell that she didn't believe shit I was saying.

"Remy Deveaux don't have me go drag her ass," she warned.

"Babe trust me, you good."

I walked back inside with this shit on my mind. I damn sure couldn't tell Skyy this shit.

Fuck.

I hope this kid ain't mine. If it was, this shit was about to be drama.

121

SKYY PEARSON

"Oooh girl this is cute." Tierra said.

"Yeah but I'm not trying to have that in my place T." I said. "That's too much. I just need some basic furniture. I'm not gonna be home like that so I don't need anything extra. And I'm definitely not trying to do anything white." I told her shaking my head at the next suggestion.

We were out shopping for furniture for my apartment. I had finally moved into my own spot after like three months of living in Tierra's spare bedroom and crashing at Remy's. Not that I was complaining, but I was happy as hell. It wasn't nothing like having my own.

I had gotten a new job working at a dental office and had been working there the last few weeks. They were paying me twenty dollars an hour. And it was full-time with benefits. It wasn't necessarily what I wanted to do for the rest of my life but it was a start. It damn sure beat working in that damn strip club.

I was happy because for the last couple of months things had been going really good. Remy and I were officially a couple and had been together for a good minute. I was a little nervous at first about jumping into another relationship, but it was literally like hanging out with my friend. And we didn't have any of the bullshit drama. Even Dymond had fell back. His boys were a mess, but even they were cool. I was trying to hook Tierra up with Remy's friend Dante. She had stopped fucking with that nigga Marcus a few weeks back so she needed a good guy. Dre was trying hard to get at her, but he had baby mama drama and every time I turned around he was having his shit tore up by his ex. I was not about to subject my bestie to that shit and I was tired of seeing her ass on Tinder and POF.

"So what you and your man doing tonight?" She asked looking at a few price tags.

"Nothing. Probably just hanging out." I shrugged walking over to some ottomans. "He said he was going to help me unpack some stuff. I really don't have much though."

"Well I'm sure he'll probably keep you laced with stuff," she smiled. "That nigga loves offering to do shit for you."

"Girl, I am not tryna have him take care of me." I told her.

"Why not?" she asked shocked. "That nigga stay jumping up to try and do whatever you want him to do. You better let him spoil your ass."

"Seriously T, think about it." I pointed out. "The last time I was with a nigga that took care of me like that, I ended up with Malachi's ass."

"Speaking of," she mentioned.

"What?" I sighed knowing it was about to be some bullshit.

"You know he hit me up on Facebook."

"For what?" I stopped looking through the catalog and looked at her.

"He said he wanted to check on you," she said. "I told him that I hadn't heard from you. But you know that nigga knew I was lying."

"Well, I don't understand why he still trying to reach out." I said flipping through the pages for something to buy. "I made it clear that we were done. I changed my number and haven't talked to him in a minute."

"Well, maybe he just wanted to check on you for real bish, I don't know," she shrugged. "Don't attack the messenger."

"Well, like I said, we ain't got shit to talk about." I repeated. "Let him control another broads life because I'm gonna have mine."

"Well while you're feeling all self-righteous and shit, can we go get something to eat because I am starving," she complained.

"Might as well. I don't really see anything I like." I sighed, placing the catalog book down and looking around the furniture store.

"We can place a special order if need be ma'am," the clerk said, obviously annoyed because I was talking shit about the merchandise in the store.

It wasn't my fault the stuff was garbage. Everything in there just looked like some stuff that you would find in a nursing home.

I ignored him and walked out of the store. We hopped in Tierra's car and headed to grab a quick bite at Panera Bread since it was close. We sat down after getting our food and chopped it up about everything that was going on.

"Oh shit." Tierra said suddenly looking behind me.

"What?" I asked wondering what was up.

"Bitch it's Malachi," she hissed. "And he with some bitch."

I followed her gaze and she was right. He was walking in with the very bitch that he had cheated on me with; Zoey. She had her hands all over him and my blood started boiling.

He saw me and his ass damn near turned green. I rolled my eyes and went back to my food while his little hoe pulled him away and walked up to the counter to order. I really didn't have time for this shit today.

"Bitch who is that?" Tierra asked.

"The bitch he was fucking when we were together." I sniped.

"I know you fucking lying," she said turning to look at her. "A white bitch? Gurrrrl…"

"I know." I gritted.

She was placing her order like she didn't have a care in the world and he kept turning to look over his shoulder at me. I was hoping he wouldn't come say anything but of course he did because he managed to pull away from her long enough to walk over to me.

"Hello Skyy," he greeted. "How have you been?"

"I'm good." I responded.

I was going to be nice because we were in these white folks establishment.

"I tried to call you," he told me. "And text you too."

"I changed my number." I stated.

"I see." He stood there looking stupid and cleared his throat. "I messaged your friend here on Facebook but she said she hadn't heard from you."

"Her friend has a name." Tierra hissed.

"Anyhoo." Malachi dismissed. "I thought maybe you would want the rest of your stuff."

"No. I think I'm okay." I told him.

"Well you look amazing," he complimented looking at me all thirsty.

"Umm...shouldn't you be getting to your little friend over there?" Tierra said looking in the direction of where he left Zoey standing.

She looked annoyed as hell seeing him talking to me. Miss Thing knew exactly who I was. I smirked seeing her expression.

"She's a coworker." Malachi told her. "That's it."

"Right..." Tierra exaggerated.

"Skyy can we please talk?" he asked, turning to me. "It's been months."

"Exactly." I nodded chewing my food. "So at this point, I don't really understand what we would have to talk about. You're a practical person. So I laid it out for you as simple as possible. I cared about you. I loved you. I loved the good times. But I can't be with somebody that won't allow me to make decisions for myself. That controlling shit is for weak minded individuals and that's not me. I'm happy where I am in life right now. I've got my own job. I got my own apartment. And I have somebody who supports me."

His eyes bucked slightly hearing me say that.

"S—s—so you've moved on already?" he stammered.

I had to admit, the shit tickled me to see him caught off guard like that. He actually looked like he was hurt. I don't know why though because he and I were over!

"Yes. I have." I nodded. "And apparently, so have you."

"So were you talking to him when we were together?" He pressed.

"Bye Malachi." I said rolling my eyes and shaking my head.

This nigga had his nerve.

"I'm sorry," he apologized. "Look I didn't mean that."

"I'm sure you did." I disagreed. "But, at this point, you should just…go."

"Okay," he said looking pitiful. "I just wanted you to know that I'm sorry." He turned to walk off but stopped and turned back to me. "Skyy, it may not mean anything but, I love you. I haven't stopped loving you. And if you want to talk—"

"There's—nothing—to—talk—about." I stopped him.

"Okay," he conceded. "I hope he makes you happy."

He walked off and I just looked at Tierra.

"Girl," she sighed looking at me agitated. "No he didn't!"

"Yes he did." I grunted. "But I ain't even gonna worry about it. Come on let's just go. I gotta get ready to go to work in a few anyway."

"Mmk," she agreed taking a gulp of her drink.

We grabbed our shit and tossed it in the trash and headed back out to the car. I was just ready to go at that point and head home. I had to go to work later on that afternoon for a couple of hours.

Tierra dropped me off to my spot and I ran inside real quick to change clothes. I hopped in my 2016 Maxima and headed to work.

I wasn't even there but an hour and I guess God just decided that today was the day to mess with me because in walked Dymond's ass. She saw me and her face just lit up.

"Wow," she smiled.

I sighed and took a deep breath. I had to calm down because I was not about to let this bitch cost me my job.

"Hello. Welcome to Mecklenburg Dental." I greeted trying to sound professional.

"Of all the dentist offices you work in this one?" she looked around.

"Here to get your mouth checked?" I said sarcastically.

126

I wanted to say a whole lot more but it was a bunch of people around.

"Actually yeah. Pregnancy causes swelling of the gums," she grinned patting her stomach.

I looked down and saw a small pooch.

"Oh you're pregnant?" I asked. This bitch was probably just fat. "Congratulations."

"Yep. I'm not that far along though. Only about six weeks," she told me. "Girl Remy is so excited about being a daddy."

I almost choked hearing his name. She knew that she had caught me off guard.

"Oh he didn't tell you?" she went on.

"Tell me what?" I fake smiled.

"Girl me and Remy are having a baby. I told you, he can't get enough of me," she giggled.

"Yeah. Okay." I nodded.

I wasn't about to let this hoe see me worried. She was probably lying anyway. She wasn't pregnant by this nigga.

"Well, I need to check in I guess so I can see the dentist?" she said interrupting me.

"Here." I said handing her a clipboard. "Fill this out and someone will call you back shortly."

She snatched the clipboard from my hand, and I watched her go sit down.

Was this bitch really pregnant by Remy? Was this shit really happening? Was I being punked?

I pulled my cell out to text Remy to call me at work. We weren't supposed to have our personal phones out while on company time.

No sooner than I hit the send button, he called.

"Mecklenburg Dental. This is Skyy."

"Hey wassup babe?" he said. "I was just thinking about you."

I didn't have time for the bullshit. I went right in on his ass.

"I have one question for you." I whispered speaking into the phone.

"What's up?" he asked.

"Did you get that bitch Dymond pregnant?"

127

He grew quiet on the phone and that was all the confirmation I needed. He lied to me. He fucked this bitch! He fucking cheated on me knowing what I had been through. With the bitch he told me I had nothing to worry about?

"Skyy...listen—"

"Fuck you!" I hissed slamming down the phone.

My co-worker Beverly turned and looked at me worried.

"Are you okay?" she asked.

"Yea." I cleared my throat and nodded. "Everything is fine."

I looked to see Dymond staring at me with an amused look on her face.

It was taking everything in me not to jump over this desk and drag her pregnant ass all over the floor.

Everything was not okay. It wasn't okay at all. I got played again. I put myself out there and I fell for a nigga that I thought would be different. He wasn't Malachi. But the fact of the matter was, he wasn't shit either.

REMY

"*This is Skyy. I can't answer my phone right now so leave a message.*"

"Skyy. Hey babe. Give me a call when you get a chance. I know you at work so you busy right now but just hit me back okay?"

I hung up the phone and headed back inside Dantes crib. We were all over there chillin and trying to figure out who was going to Atlanta to bring some bricks in. When Skyy told me that she needed me to call her, I wasn't expecting for her to ask me about Dymond. How the hell did she find out about that shit anyway? Now she wasn't answering the phone and I didn't know what was going on.

I thought about calling her at work, but I didn't want to get her in trouble.

"Shit!" I said walking back inside.

"Yo nigga what's up with you?" Dre asked when I came in.

"Man I just got off the phone with Skyy." I said flopping down on the couch.

"Yea aight?"

"Bruh I don't know how she found out, but she knows about Dymond and her being pregnant." I said .

I was rubbing my head because I could feel a headache coming on.

"Oh shit." Dante mumbled. "Yo, you sure she know bruh?"

"My nigga, her exact words were, *'Did you get that bitch Dymond pregnant'.* So she knows."

"Well nigga I already told you that I don't think shawty pregnant by you anyway." Dre spoke up. "Nigga you know how that hoe is."

"Yea well right now the only thing I'm thinking about is my girl man. I tried to talk to her and she just hung up."

"So what you gone do?" Dante asked.

"I gotta go holla at her about this shit man." I sighed. "See what all she know."

"Well go handle your business my nigga. We can handle shit here." Dante assured me.

"You gone have to do the pick up." I told him.

"I got you." Dante nodded.

"Aye, when you go holla at Skyy, see what's up with her homegirl." Dre said.

I looked at that nigga like he was stuck on stupid.

"See, this is why Dante handling this shit." I said. "Really nigga?"

"What? I'm just saying," he shrugged. "Shit ole girl is bad as hell."

Even though I was stressed the fuck out, leave it to Dre to have a nigga ready to laugh.

"Yo I'm out." I told them. "Dre keep your eyes open."

"Fa sho," he confirmed.

That nigga may have been off and a dumb ass at times but he was a fucking sharp shooter.

I left out hoping this pick up went off without a hitch and headed to Skyy's spot. I just wanted to talk to her and find out what was going on.

How the hell did she find out about Dymond being pregnant? Dymond's ass didn't talk to her like that. Who the fuck told her?

Something told me to hit up Dymond's ass. She had something to do with this shit. I knew she did. I just didn't know how. But I was about to find out.

I called her phone to see if she would answer but it went to voicemail.

"Yo, hit me back when you get this message." I said. "We need to talk. ASAP."

I was close to Skyy's house and I was nervous as hell. I didn't know what she knew or what she had heard. She had never really tripped out on me like that before. I had to fix this shit. I knew I should have said something in the beginning. Shit!

I pulled into her complex and parked. She hadn't gotten home yet so I let myself in. She was only working a few hours that day so I knew she would be home soon.

I sat on her couch and called Dymond a few more times but she didn't answer. I sat and waited for Skyy for what seemed like hours.

When she finally walked through the door and saw me sitting there, I knew she was pissed off and it was about to be some shit.

"Why are you here?" She spat dropping her bag and crossing her arms.

"Because we need to talk." I answered.

"Yeah we need to talk alright," she said.

"Well you hung up before I could say anything." I reasoned.

"What the hell do I need to hear that you gotta say Remy?" she shrieked. "You got this bitch pregnant. You didn't say that you didn't. So we ain't got shit to talk about. Your ass was out there fucking around on me with that bitch, all the while you looking me in my face and telling me I'm good. But then this bitch shows up to my job and tells me how she's having your baby and shit."

"Okay but babe I promise you I just found out." I tried to interject.

"Oh shut that shit up!" she barked. "You didn't just find out. That's a bunch of bullshit. You lied. You cheated. You know what the fuck I went through with Malachi's ass and you turn around and do the same thing?"

"Skyy wasn't nobody fucking around on you." I told her. "I ain't fuck that girl since we got together. Me and her was just fucking around every now and then but I told you that."

"Remy please!" she stressed. "You honestly expect me to believe you? Your—baby—mama—showed—up—to—my—job—and—told—me—she—was—pregnant!"

She was clapping her hands and screaming. I had never seen her little ass so worked up before. I was trying to talk but she just kept going the fuck off.

"This bitch shows up to my job talking about how she's six weeks pregnant and shit," she ranted. "We been together for damn near three months and you got her cheesing all in my face making me look stupid where I work."

"Yo she lying!" I blurted out.

"No nigga you the one that's fucking lying!" she cried. "Remy you got that bitch pregnant! You said it yourself so how the hell is she lying about that? How you think that shit made me feel? Huh? She come strolling up in my job, rubbing her belly and telling me that y'all are just so excited because y'all are having this fucking baby."

"Skyy! Listen to me!" I stopped her. "Baby I did not cheat on you. The last time I fucked her was before me and you got together. Me and you had only fucked around one time and yea I was still fucking with her but I swear I did not cheat on you." I explained. "I just found out that night at the club. She showed me the fucking ultrasound. I don't know why the fuck she told you she was only six weeks but she told me something else. I swear."

She sniffed and looked down at the ground. I walked over to her and tried to hold her but she snatched away from me.

"No Remy," she sniffed. "I can't believe you. I don't believe anything that you say. When she came to my job and she stood in my face and told me she was having your baby, I was devastated. But then when I talked to you on the phone and I asked you if it was true..."

Her eyes watered with tears and I could tell she was trying to hold it together.

"Baby—" I whispered. "Why would I do that to you? I didn't say anything because I didn't think it was my baby. I wanted to find out first. I figured if it wasn't mine, then I wouldn't have to say anything to you about it."

"So what if it was yours huh?" she challenged. "What if she hadn't come in my job today? What were you going to do? Just spring it on me?"

"I don't know." I admitted reaching out for her again.

"Just—stop," she said. "Remy I—I can't do this."

"Skyy, you know you've been the only one that I've cared about and wanted like that since Nikki." I confessed. "I have never felt this way about anybody the way I have you."

"Well if this is how you show it Remy, then I don't want it."

She moved away from me and sat down on the couch. I was about to walk over to her but she stopped me.

"You need to go," she whispered. "I just—I can't deal with this right now, so you need to go. Please."

"Skyy will you just—"

"No!" she jumped up. "No I won't listen to you. I'm done with that. Remy I told you, I'm not about to be one of these bitches that's letting her man cheat on her and she just takes it. I'm not built like that. I've dealt with that shit with Malachi and I'm not doing it again. So you and Dymond and y'alls baby can have a happy life. Cause I'm out."

She walked over to the door and opened it.

"Skyy...baby...don't do something that you're gonna regret." I told her.

"The only thing I regret right now is meeting you," she said. "Bye."

I walked past her and walked out of the door.

"You just don't know what kind of man I am." I told her.

"I'm sure Nikki didn't know either," she said. "And look where it got her."

Hearing her say that shit infuriated me but she closed the door in my face before I could react. I walked down the stairs and out of the building.

Her bringing up my ex pissed me the fuck off. She didn't know Nikki and I wasn't about to let Skyy disrespect her in any way. Fuck all this shit. I wasn't about to deal with the bullshit and for damn sure didn't have time for it. If she didn't wanna believe me, then fuck it. Fuck her!

I got in the car and started to head home. Fuck it. I was going to ride to Atlanta and get this bread. I thought about Dymond. She was the reason for all this bullshit. Why the fuck would she go and tell

Skyy some crazy shit like that? And why the fuck did Skyy just believe whatever the fuck this bitch told her? This bitch was really starting to get on my nerves. These sick ass fucking games that she was playing was about to end. I was going to stop this shit before I went anywhere else.

I busted a U-turn and headed to her house. She lived like 15 minutes away. I got there and started banging on the door.

"What the hell?" I heard her say from the other side. She yanked the door open and looked at me with a wild and crazed expression. "What the fuck are you doing here?"

"Yo who is it?" I heard.

I stormed in pushing past her and some nigga was coming out the bedroom in his draws.

"Aye my nigga, if you don't want to get your ass fucked up, you need to raise the fuck up out of here." I warned.

"Uh uh nigga you just don't walk up in my house acting like you running shit," she yelled.

"Shut the fuck up!" I barked. "You wouldn't have this shit if it wasn't for me."

"Aye patna you ain't talking to my baby mama like that," this lil nigga threatened.

He walked over to me like he was really about to do some shit. I almost picked him up and body slammed him but my beef was with Dymond's ass.

"Your baby mama? Oh word?" I said turning to her. "Because if you let this bitch tell it...I'm the muthafucking baby daddy."

I watched her mouth drop open and I knew she had this dumb ass nigga really thinking he was the father and shit. I walked over to her and snatched her ass.

"I don't know what the fuck your problem is." I gritted. "I told you before, I'm fucking done with you. So quit coming at my girl with that bullshit. You got her thinking that I been fucking with your ass this whole goddamn time."

"Man get the fuck off her!" this little nigga yelled.

He had to be 150 pounds soaking wet and actually tried to swing on me.

"Muthafucka!" I growled, turning around to knock his ass out.

I snatched him and hit him square in the face, watching him fall to the ground. I started stomping him in the face and Dymond was screaming begging me to stop.

"You're gonna kill him!" she screamed.

"Good! Stupid ass nigga!" I kept stomping. "Wanna try me bitch? Talk that shit now nigga!"

I punched and stomped that nigga until he stopped moving.

"Stop!" she cried.

I was trying to catch my breath when I realized I probably just killed his ass. I looked at her and it was taking everything in me not to choke her the fuck out.

"Be clear. I don't wanna hear from you until this fucking baby is born." I told her. "Don't you say another fucking word to my girl. Don't even look in her direction. Don't be tryna stir up no more bullshit. Stay the fuck away for me and mine. Or I promise you that you gone get worse than your boy over there."

I walked out slamming the door behind me and could hear her crying. I didn't give a fuck. I wasn't about to let this broad fuck up the bit of happiness that I had.

But a nigga didn't even know if I had it anymore.

REMY

"Remy Jaylin Deveaux, what in the world is the matter with you?"

"What are you talking about? I'm good."

"You a good lie," my mother stated. "The whole time we were in church, your head was somewhere else. Now you know I don't fuss at you about going to church like that even though I think your little behind needs to be in that pew every Sunday, especially with what you got going on."

"Mama—"

"Aht aht! Don't you interrupt me boy!" she fussed. "Now I'm not stupid Remy. I birthed you. So I know that your little behind is out here in the streets. Now you're a grown man and I can't stop you from doing what you wanna do. If I could, your behind would be in church every day of the week. No. All I can do is pray that you don't get locked up or dead. That's why I'm always trying to get you to go to church with me so maybe you can realize what it is that you're doing and stop. But ain't no point in you going to church if your mind is gonna be somewhere else. Now what in the world is going on?" She said as she finished fixing a plate and putting it in front of me.

I was at my mother's house after leaving church. She always tried to get me to go with her by making me feel guilty at least once a month. But I agreed to go today because Nikki's mother was supposed to be coming by.

"Ma, there's nothing." I told her.

"Did you just hear me say that I birthed you boy?" she said. "Now I'ma ask you one more time what's wrong so stop lying and spill it. Who is she?"

"Huh?" I said lifting my head up from my plate.

"Remy!" she screeched.

"Her name is Skyy." I caved.

"Uh huh," she said pulling out a chair from the table and sitting down. "Well she gotta be something to have you over here with your head in the clouds looking like you in a New Edition 'Can You Stand the Rain' video."

I couldn't help but to smile at my mom's joke. She knew me well.

"So what did you do?" She asked.

"Now why I got to do something wrong?" I asked shoving some food in my mouth.

She gave me that mama look and I sighed knowing she wasn't going to let this go.

"It wasn't anything like that." I said. "But me and Skyy had been kicking it and she found out that I might have another girl pregnant."

"You what!" she yelled clutching her pearls. "Remy, don't you play with me. What do you mean you got some girl pregnant?"

"Ma relax." I tried to calm her down. "I don't know for sure. But there was a girl that I was hanging out with before Skyy and well... I don't know." I shrugged, taking a gulp of my water. "It could be but I don't think it is."

"So, you out here messing with two girls at one time?" she questioned. "What, you trying to be like your father now?"

"No." I shook my head. I hated when she compared me to him. She had her feelings about my pops but that was some shit between them. But I needed her to hear me. "Ma, I was kicking it with this girl before I met Skyy."

"And who is this other woman?"

"Her name is Dymond." I replied.

"Oh Lord," she said throwing up her hands and getting up. "Please tell me she's not a stripper."

I just kept my mouth shut because that was going to open up a whole other can of worms. The doorbell rang thank God and my mom tossed her towel down so she could go answer it.

"Hey Gloria!" I heard her say.

I kept eating grateful that Ms. Gloria had shown up so that my mama could lay off of me for a while. A few seconds later they walked into the kitchen where I was and Ms. Gloria walked right over to me and gave me a big hug.

"Hey Remy baby," she smiled. "How are you doing?"

"I'm doing good Ms. G." I told her giving her a tight squeeze.

I loved her like a second mother. Even though Nikki was gone, I still kept in touch with her to make sure that she was straight. She never wanted for anything.

"Gloria why don't you go ahead and take you a seat. I'll fix you a plate," mama offered. "I'm just sitting here fussing at this son of mine about this possible baby that he got."

I almost choked when she said that. I looked at Ms. Gloria and she looked at me waiting for answers.

"Now I know you not out here just having sex unprotected are you?" She asked.

"No ma'am."

"Apparently you are," my mama said. "Chile he over here sulking in church looking all pitiful because his little girlfriend don't want to deal with him now that he got a baby."

"Damn it ma—"

"Boy you better watch your mouth!" she fussed.

"Yes ma'am." I mumbled ducking my head down.

That was the last thing that I needed was for Ms. G to know what was going on. She was the mother of my first love. How could I talk to her about this?

"Remy?" she questioned.

"Yes ma'am?" I said slowly.

"Are you okay baby?" she asked.

"Yes ma'am." I nodded. "I just—I didn't really want to tell you."

I cut my eyes at my mother but she wasn't fazed at all.

"Remy please," my mother spoke. "Nikki's been gone for a while now. You really think that Gloria is going to hold it over you if you moved on and got into a relationship? Hell I was wondering when you were going to finally settle down my damn self. Clearly, I wish I had known about it before you went out here and started spreading your seed everywhere. But, it's okay."

I looked at Ms. Gloria and she nodded in agreement taking my hand.

"It really is okay baby," she whispered. "Your mother is right. Now you know I love you like a son, but Nikki is gone. My granddaughter, she's gone. And it's not like they can come back. Nikki would want you to be happy and you know that."

"Yes ma'am." I said nodding my head, trying to swallow the lump in my throat.

"Listen, you deserve to be happy. But look here, don't be out here making all these babies," she said playfully thumping me on my forehead.

"Yes ma'am." I laughed.

"Do you want to be with this girl?" She asked me.

"Yes." I told her. "She's different than any girl I've ever met. Like she's real cool. She smart too. And I don't know but she just really makes me think about things differently. From the first day I met her, I couldn't get her out of my head. And trust me I tried. But, then I got this mess with Dymond. And I don't want to be with her."

"Oh but you just making babies with her though right?" my mother chimed in.

"Mama I don't even know if it's mine or not." I confessed. "I'm not saying it isn't because I know that I did some stupid stuff and didn't necessarily wear condoms like I was supposed to but I don't know."

"Well, first things first is you need to have a conversation with this

Dymond girl and find out when you can get a paternity test," she suggested. "And then if you really want to be with this girl, Skyy? Then you better go over there and beg her for forgiveness. And you can't get mad if she doesn't want to deal with you no more." She sat down on the other side of me and looked at me serious. "You have to understand how that girl feels right now. A baby? By somebody you weren't even with? And you didn't tell her anything? Keeping something from somebody is worse than lying to somebody. It feels like they're being cheated on."

"I know ma." I admitted.

"Good," she smiled. "You know I'm not gonna sugarcoat anything for you. I'm your mama and I'm gonna tell you what you need to hear, not what you want to hear."

I smiled and hugged her. We all sat back and talked for a while and eventually I got ready to leave. I was going to go try to talk to Skyy like my mother suggested. This shit had gone on long enough and I missed her. Skyy was everything. She was the total package. Everything about her was dope. And I wasn't about to lose her because of Dymond's ass. If it was my baby, I would be there for the child but that was it.

I gave my mom a kiss and promised to check in with Ms. Gloria soon and headed over to Skyy's. I was hopeful when I saw her car outside. I jogged up the steps pulling out my key and hoping that she hadn't changed the locks. I stopped seeing some bougie uppity looking nigga standing at her door holding flowers. He looked at me as I was coming up the steps and turned back around like I wasn't there.

"Yo who you?" I asked.

"Malachi Jackson," he said looking at me nervous like I was going to rob him. "I'm here to see my girlfriend."

"Skyy?"

"Yes," he nodded. "I'm sorry, who are you? How do you know her?"

The door opened and Skyy stood at the entrance.

"Malachi?" She said.

"Hello sweetheart," he greeted leaning forward and kissing her.

I came up the rest of the stairs and she saw me. Her eyes got big like she was caught.

"Remy? What are you doing here?" she questioned.

I wanted to whoop her nigga ass but I wasn't about to waste my energy on this nigga. If this is what she wanted, cool.

"It doesn't even matter no more." I told her. "I'll holla at you later."

I turned and walked down the steps not even giving a fuck. She wanted to be with that cornball ass nigga after all that shit she talked about not wanting somebody controlling her and all that? But this nigga was at her door.

Getting in my car, I just sat there. I was mad. I ain't gonna lie. I had hyped myself up to come over here and apologize but she had already moved on. I wasn't about to chase her.

My phone started ringing and I looked to see Dymond calling.

"What?" I answered cranking the truck and leaving the parking lot.

"Hey. I was wondering if we could talk," she said.

"About what?" I asked.

"Well, I was hoping that we could talk face to face and be civil but I can hear attitude bouncing off you," she observed. I could hear her breathing deep. "Look Remy I'm really scared and I'm hormonal and all this crazy shit with this pregnancy."

I sighed knowing it was about to be some mess. Shit. I'd be glad when I find out if this was my baby or not.

"Look, give me fifteen minutes. I'll be there." I told her finally.

"Okay," she sniffed.

I drove my truck in the direction of her crib hoping that I could deal with her crazy ass. I was trying to block the images of Malachi's ass standing at Skyy's door out of my mind. Here I was trying to do shit to be with her and she had already moved on. Fuck it. I didn't even care anymore.

I got to Dymond's place and she opened the door before I could even knock.

"Damn were you sitting there looking out the window waiting on me to pull up?"

"Something like that," she said meekly. "I had gone to check the mail and I saw your truck coming up the street."

"Dressed like that?"

I looked at her standing in front of me with this silk robe on. Her stomach was sticking out. It was more obvious now that she was pregnant.

I flopped down on her sofa while she closed the door. She came and sat down next to me.

"What's the matter with you?" she asked.

"Nothing." I answered. I damn sure wasn't about to talk to her about my problems with Skyy. Hell nah. "What did you wanna talk about?"

"Remy I'll be six months in a week. And for the most part, I've just dealt with this by myself," she said. "I know that I haven't been the easiest person but I wanted to know if you could be here through this pregnancy. I mean, I'm in my second trimester now and I don't want to go through the rest of this alone."

She was teary eyed and I could tell she was trying not to cry in front of me.

"I mean, you know how I feel on this." I told her.

"I know. And Remy like I said, we can get the DNA test done. That's how confident I am that it's yours," she urged. "I'm not out here just fucking with niggas like that despite what you may think."

I was going to bring up the nigga that was here the last time but decided against it. I could see that she was trying to be sincere and shit.

"Aight." I told her. "I ain't saying that I'm gonna be there holding your hand or anything like that but the next time you got an appointment just let me know. I'll be there."

"Really?" She smiled eagerly.

"Yeah." I answered.

"Thank you," she cooed throwing herself on me.

She was jumping around like a little kid. She landed in my lap and instinctively I grabbed her around her waist. Her ass was sitting right on my dick. I guess that pregnancy shit was accurate because she was looking good. Even though I was mad, my dick still knew what was up.

She looked at me and I knew what she wanted. I was going to give it to her. I wasn't with Skyy anymore. Fuck it. Might as well go back to the old me.

SKYY

"Okay Skyy, you've been sulking in this apartment now for like the last four or five weeks. If you're not gonna talk to the nigga, then at least go out and do something. Like damn you acting like somebody's old ass grandma right now."

"I'm tired." I argued with Tierra. "I'm just—I'm really not trying to go nowhere."

"But why though?"

"Because I just don't want to okay?" I sighed. "I just wanna lay here. I don't want to risk running into his ass."

"Girl, it's Charlotte. You act like he right next door or something," she fussed. "Come on. Get up. Let's go to Epic Centre. We can go to a club. Something."

"I'm sorry T. I'm just not really up to going out like that honestly." I told her.

I really wasn't. Since Remy and I broke up, all I was doing was going to work, coming home, and getting ready to start the next school semester; which is exactly why Tierra was over at my house in my face. She was trying to get me to go out to celebrate my enrollment at school.

It wasn't like I was actually going to a school on campus. I was doing online classes at Liberty University. I was majoring in Business Administration.

"Come on. You need to celebrate," she nagged. "It's not every day that I can say my bestie is going to college! That's a big deal Skyy."

"Not really." I shrugged laying on the couch. "I mean, I'm excited, don't get me wrong. But, it's not really the real experience and all of that. I wanna go to like Johnson C. Smith or maybe UNC Charlotte but I'm too old to be on the campus doing all of that so...at least this way I can still work and get my degree."

"That's wassup," she nodded. "But still Skyy, that doesn't mean that you got to be sitting here doing nothing either. You're about to be twenty-four years old and you sitting in the house on a Friday night like you in your seventies or something. You sitting here like you got a husband. some bad ass kids and no life. I don't understand. I thought you said that you were okay since y'all split?"

"I mean I am." I sighed. "I mean I think I am. I'm just—I guess I'm just tired."

"Have you talked to him?" she asked.

"No." I shook my head. "He was calling me for a while but he stopped."

"I don't blame his ass. You were being way too mean," she fussed flipping the channel on the TV.

"Excuse me?" I said turning to look at her.

"I'm just saying Skyy. I really think you need to ease up on Remy," she advised. "It's not like y'all were really deep into the relationship. I mean yeah y'all had only been together for a couple of months. And technically, he had been fucking with her before you. He said that she lied about how far along she was and you saw that for yourself when he showed you the ultrasound in the text message."

"Yeah but still T, he lied and didn't tell me that she was pregnant. He kept that from me." I reminded her. "I don't want to be dealing with somebody like that and I don't know what's going on behind closed doors."

"I get it," she agreed. "I know I would be mad too. But I'm just saying that I think that you might be...you know...being a little to hard on him. Dante and I were talking and—"

"Wait...since when did you start talking to Dante?" I asked.

"Girl, quit trying to change the subject. That's my business," she rushed.

"Nah. Uh uh." I said sitting up interested and snatching the remote out of her hand. "I wanna talk about you and this Dante thing. When did that happen?"

"A few weeks ago," she told me sighing. "I didn't want to say anything because we're just getting to know each other."

"Oh really? Hmm..."

"Don't start," she warned.

"I'm not saying nothing." I gave up.

"Well like I was saying, Dante and I were talking and I just don't think you should be so hard on Remy," she went on. "He's not Malachi. He's not tryna control you or anything like that. And after everything you told me about his girl passing away and him not being in a relationship with nobody since then, obviously he's saying that there is something in you that's different. You're special to him. So talk to him."

"I can't." I argued. "I just—I don't know. I can't go back and be looking stupid. He lied T."

"Okay yea, he should've told you," she agreed. "I'll give you that. But damn. Can you blame him? He's apologized. He showed you proof the bitch was lying. So why are you still punishing him?"

"Look T, just leave it alone okay?" I urged. "You wouldn't understand."

"Oh I understand," she shook her head. "I understand that your ass is stubborn and don't want to call him. I understand that nigga wanna be with you. I understand his ass is just as miserable as your ass is."

"Well can you understand how to be quiet?" I cut her off. "Can you understand how to mind your own business?"

She looked at me and scrunched up her nose.

"Okay. I wont say another word," she conceded. "But I'm just saying, you gone fuck around and he gone get snatched up by some other chic."

"Okay?" I shrugged.

I didn't care. Some other chic could have him. I wasn't about to worry about another nigga.

"You know what? I ain't even gonna talk about it cause your ass ain't gone listen no way," she gave up. "You just gonna keep doing whatever you wanna do and sitting here in this house like some old ass lady wallowing and feeling miserable. And if you keep eating all that damn junk, your ass is going to be fat as hell."

"Okay Tierra." I sighed rolling my eyes. "Look, you don't understand what I'm going through okay?"

"I don't understand?" She asked.

She snatched the remote out of my hand and turned the TV off.

"Look Skyy, this is me being real with you right now," she stood in front of me. "You don't think I understand how it feels to be liking somebody or caring about somebody and they completely just crush you? Hurt you? You don't think that I understand that? Now, I may not have liked Malachi, and Lord knows he was a complete bitch but I was happy for you. Because I knew that you deserved to be happy. I watched my friend be happy; for the most part and wondered why I couldn't have that."

She looked down at me and I could see she was getting choked up.

"You think I'm just out here dating niggas just to date em? You think I like starting over every few weeks or months or whatever and feeling like there's something wrong with me?" she continued. "No. I want happiness too. The only difference is, the niggas that I'm trying to be with, when they crush me, they're not worried about how I feel. They could care less. But you got a man that wants to be with you. You got a man that is trying hard to show you that he wants you. You got a nigga that everybody knows and everybody wants and he ain't even thinking about them. But you just completely shut him out. Yeah that nigga fucked up big time by not telling you about that bitch being pregnant. But damn. It wasn't like he cheated. Like you know he didn't cheat. You know how vindictive that bitch is. But you're still making him suffer. Why? I just don't get it. If it was me, yeah, I would have made him feel bad a little bit. And yeah I might've been petty for a minute. But, I'm not about to let the next bitch get what's mine. I'm not about to let her win. But I guess that's the difference between me and you."

I knew she was right. But how can I go back to him? How could I just act like everything was cool? The shit still hurt. That was the part that seemed like nobody wanted to understand.

"Look T..." I huffed sitting up and straightening my clothes. "It's not like I don't miss him okay? I do. And it's not like I don't want to be with him because I do. But I'm just scared that if I take him back after all of this, what if he decides to keep something else from me? What if next time he's not sorry or he just expects me to take it?"

"Then that's where you let his ass know what's up!" she expressed. "You take control Skyy. You let that nigga know what you're not going to deal with. And if that nigga really care about you like I know he do, then it's not gonna be a problem for him."

"I guess." I sighed.

"Just think about it," she suggested. "Now I got to get ready to go because I got to go to work tonight. But, I'll come by and check on you in a little bit?"

"Yup." I nodded.

She hugged me and left. I laid back down on the couch thinking about everything. I really did miss Remy. But it had been so long.

Was he even still thinking about me? I hadn't heard from him in weeks. At first, he was calling me all the time but that stopped. Now I just didn't know what to think. I needed to get out of the house. I had wallowed in this shit long enough.

I got up and took a shower and put on some clothes. I was doing my hair when I heard a knock at the door. Walking to the front I looked out the peephole and frowned.

"What the fuck?" I mumbled.

I opened the door and was completely surprised.

"Malachi?"

"Hello sweetheart," he smiled stepping forward and kissing me on the lips.

This muthafucka actually wrapped his arms around me to hug me. But what caught me all the way off guard was who I saw standing behind him coming up the stairs.

"Remy?" I froze. "What are you doing here?"

The way he looked at me I knew he was hurt.

"It don't even matter no more," he said. "I'll holla at you later."

He just turned and walked off like it was nothing.

"Wait." I called after him but he kept going.

I watched him walk down the stairs before turning back to Malachi who was standing in front of me. He was dressed in a polo shirt and khakis holding flowers.

"What the hell are you doing here Malachi?"

"Skyy. I was hoping that we can talk. I wanted to come to you and see about us trying to work this out. Here," he said. "I got you these."

He was standing in my doorway with these long stem roses he was trying to give me. Normally that would have made my heart melt but now, getting them from him, it just made my stomach churn. I took them from him faking a smile and then chunked them bitches down the stairs.

"Skyy—" he yelped as his mouth dropped open.

"No. First of all, you don't just pop the fuck up at my house." I started. "Secondly, how the fuck did you even find out where I live?"

He stood looking like the little weasel that he was and mumbled.

"I hired a private investigator to follow you after I saw you at Panera Bread," he explained.

"You what?!" I screamed. "You hired a fucking private investigator?"

"Yes," he admitted. "But it was the only thing I could think of. I really wanted to see you."

"Do you hear how crazy you sound?" I spat. "You fucking hired a goddamn private investigator! You found out where I live and then you just show up with some funky ass flowers talking about you want to work things out? Are you out of your goddamn mind?"

"Skyy there's no need to yell," he said walking towards me.

"I have every reason to yell! Your ass isn't getting it. It's over Malachi!" I screeched. "I don't want to be with you anymore. We haven't been together for months now and in case you haven't noticed, I'm doing my own thing. For once in my life, I'm doing me."

"And this is what you call doing you?" He said looking around. "Some small cramped apartment, and a used clunker of a car?"

"Oh you have really got to be fucking kidding me." I seethed. I was about to knock his ass smooth out. "How dare you come to my doorstep with that bullshit? You know, it amazes me how fucking self-righteous your ass is. I can't believe that I had ever dealt with you. But, I know one thing, not again. Malachi, get this through that thick head of yours." I licked my lips and took a deep breath before I started. "We have nothing left to discuss. You've disrespected me so much. You treated me like shit. You treated me like I was your child instead of your girlfriend. All these fucking rules that I had to follow. I'm not doing it no more. I don't want to be with you."

"You really don't wanna be with me?" He questioned.

"I—don't—wanna—be—with—you!" I screamed! "Why can't you get that shit?"

"But you'd much rather be with that little drug dealer that was here?"

"Excuse me?" I said.

Did this nigga really have the audacity to come at me on this dumb shit?

"The guy who just left after you answered the door? I know exactly who he is," he said. "I told you I had a private investigator watching you the last couple of days. I know about you working at the dental office. I know about you going to school online. Everything."

"Malachi, for your sake, you need to leave." I warned. "Get your lying, cheating, narcissistic ass the fuck out of my apartment."

"Baby wait," he said grabbing my hand. "I'm sorry. I know the way that I went about things is probably messed up. I shouldn't have had you followed. But I was desperate. I had to do something to get you. That's how much I love you. We're supposed to be together. I was supposed to propose to you last week. I don't wanna start over."

"No you'd much rather I sit at home while you go fuck these white bitches at your job." I told him. "You telling me that you have nothing to do with her but then when I do see you after we broke up who else would you be with but that same bitch. The only reason that you want me to come back is so that you don't have to start over with your little life plans. Your parents want you to be married at a certain age and your grown ass is too afraid to tell them no. Your grown ass does any and everything that they tell you to do. If you want to be their puppet that's fine. But I'm not about to be a part of his damn sick ass fucking movie."

I laughed thinking about it.

"You know being with you was like being in the movie Get Out. Like I felt like I had drank the Kool-Aid. But not anymore." I said. "Because I came to realize that your ass is not normal. Normal people don't have their ex-girlfriend's followed. Normal people don't stifle their girlfriend's creativity. Normal people don't cheat on their girl-friends. Normal people don't control their women. Normal people give a fuck about how a girl feels. But you're not normal. You're an asinine, controlling, vindictive, narcissistic trifling ass motherfucker." I pointed out. "No matter how you may dress, talk, walk, whatever. All you care about is you; Malachi."

"That's not true," he argued. "If I didn't care about you, do you think I would be here right now? Yes Skyy, I fucked up okay? I messed up bad. I will admit it. Yes, I slept with Zoey. Not because I wanted to. But because I got a little drunk, and because her father is connected. And I've been thinking about leaving the firm—"

"Stop!" I snapped. "Just stop. Do you hear yourself? Are you fucking serious? Like is that seriously the best excuse that you could come up with? You were thinking about leaving the firm? Sooo…. you slept with a bitch because of a job? But you have the nerve to stand here and judge me while you're pimping yourself out? Malachi come on. You got to come better than that."

"Skyy I'm telling the truth!" he stressed.

"And I'm supposed to believe it now?" I scoffed. "As compared to all the times that you lied to me? You had this bitch calling your phone all hours of the night and telling me that I was trippin. No! You slept with this bitch and had the nerve to flaunt her in my damn face. You were trying to control me but really you should've been controlling your damn self."

"Skyy, I didn't come here to argue," he sighed.

"I don't know what the fuck you came here for." I said. "But I know it's time for you to go. Now."

I marched to the door and yanked it open so that he could leave. He looked at me looking like some sad ass puppy all defeated and shit but I didn't care. Hearing him tell me that he fucked Zoey gave me the confirmation that I had made the right decision to leave his ass.

"Skyy please," he said grabbing me by the hand. "Don't do this."

"I ain't got nothing else to say to you." I growled. "Goodbye Malachi."

I snatched away from him and started to walk away. I grabbed my keys and slammed my door locking it behind me. I needed to get the hell out of here otherwise I didn't know what I was going to do.

"Skyy I'm on my knees begging," he pleaded.

I walked down the stairs and turned to see him on his knees. I smirked and walked back up the few steps and looked down at him.

"This is the position that you should've been in a long time ago." I sneered. "For the first time I can honestly say that I'm better than you. You are beneath me. You know that? You can have all the money in the world, but you will never have another woman like me ever again. Don't call me. Don't come to my house. Don't so much as even send me a message, email, nothing. I'm good on you."

I turned to walk off and he grabbed me wrapping his arms around me causing me to lose my balance. I fell and rolled down two flights of stairs. Everything got so dizzy. I could hear Malachi call my name and it sounded like an echo. I tried to open my mouth but tasted blood.

"Skyy." I heard. "Oh God! Oh God!"

I knew I was losing consciousness because his voice sounded distant and everything was blurred. The last thing I remember seeing before everything went black was Malachi looking at me in a panic and running off.

REMY

"Yo, what the fuck is going on with them niggas over there on Tryon? Every time I pull up, they standing around looking stupid like it ain't no money to be made." I snapped. "Niggas think I'm fucking playing with them yo. I'm gone have to body one of these niggas."

"We told them niggas to have they shit right because we coming to collect tomorrow." Dre told me.

"Nah fuck that. I ain't waiting til tomorrow. I wanna see what these niggas is up to. We pulling up on they asses tonight." I barked. "We catch them niggas slipping and figure out what the fuck they doing. I ain't got time to be dealing with the bullshit. That nigga Jay gone come to me and ask me to put him on. Now these niggas is being lazy and shit. If this nigga can't handle business, I don't need him. He's slowing my shit down."

"I feel you my nigga." Dante agreed looking up from texting somebody on his phone. "You know I'm ready to pull up."

I nodded in agreement. I was sick of letting niggas slide with shit. Right now, this was all I needed to focus on. I was done with the going back and forth between Skyy and Dymond. The shit was taking me away from making this money. I wasn't about to let this shit distract me more than it already had.

I was out on the block with Dante and Dre handling business after leaving Dymond's house. I ended up going over there after I left Skyy's house and fucked around and smashed her ass again. Now her goofy ass was right back on the same shit. She was trying to play chill, but she had already texted me three times since I left. I know I told her I was going to be there for her but I wasn't trying to be *her* boyfriend. I still didn't trust her. Especially after that shit she pulled with that nigga that I pulled up on. She had this nigga thinking it was his baby and shit but calling me? Nah. I wasn't about to be played like that. I just fucked her because I couldn't deal with that Skyy shit.

But Skyy's face was all I saw the whole time. This shit had me bugged the way she was in my head like this. How the fuck was she just going to go back to that nigga? The same nigga she said she would never even talk to again. The same nigga that she said broke her heart and lied to her. But that same nigga was at her doorstep. That nigga was a lame. He looked like he needed to read instructions to fuck. The shit was crazy to me. This was exactly why my ass was going to just be single from now on. Skyy had got in my head, but I wasn't about to make that mistake again. As far as I was concerned, that relationship shit was for the birds.

"Aye my nigga did you hear what I said?"

"What?" I said turning back to Dante.

"Yo you good my bruh?" he asked.

"Yeah I'm straight. Just let them niggas know that I'm coming to see them." I ordered.

My phone rang and I looked down at the screen to see a number that I didn't recognize.

"Yo." I answered.

"Hey is this Remy?"

"Yea." I said. "Who this?"

"Hey it's Tierra. Skyy's best friend," she announced.

"How'd you get my number?" I asked.

"I went through Skyy's phone," she explained. "I was gonna call you from her phone but her battery is low and honestly...I didn't know if you would answer after y'all broke up and everything but—look she was just brought into the hospital."

"Okay, so what you telling me for? She got a man."

"Huh? She got a—what? What the hell are you talking about?" she stressed. "Did you not just hear me say that Skyy is in the hospital? She's hurt Remy. Bad. I don't know what all happened but they told me that she's unconscious. You were the only person that I could think to call! She doesn't have any family and I wasn't gonna call Malachi. And I'm scared because I don't know what's happening."

She was babbling and crying hard and I couldn't make out what she was saying.

"Okay, okay. Calm down. Just...tell me what hospital she at."

She rattled off something I strained to hear and hung up assuring her I was coming.

Dante and Dre looked at me confused.

"Bruh what the fuck is going on with you?" Dre asked. "What, your baby mama went into labor?"

"Nah." I shook my head. "Skyy in the hospital."

"Oh shit." Dre mumbled. "My bad."

"Yo, go handle your business bruh." Dante told me. "We can hold off on that other bullshit."

"Nah." I shook my head. "That shit still gotta get handled. I'ma run up here real quick and see what's good and then we gon handle that shit. Plus we gotta drive to the A and re-up so I ain't got time to waste."

"Aight. We'll stick to the plan," he nodded.

I headed towards my truck and hopped in to go to the hospital. I hoped Tierra wasn't on no bullshit. I didn't think that she would lie about no serious shit like that but still, I didn't put shit past anybody.

I thought about my mother and called her back. She had something that she had wanted to talk to me about so I figured I'd get it out the way.

"It's about time you called me back," she answered the phone. "I'd hate it if I was hurt or it was an emergency."

"My bad Ma." I apologized. "I got caught up with some stuff."

"Mmhmm," she mumbled. "Where are you?"

"On my way to the hospital." I told her.

"What? Oh my God are you okay? What's wrong?" she rattled off.

"No Ma it's not me." I calmed her down. "I'm fine."

"Oh. Well then why are you going to the hospital?" she asked.

"It's Skyy." I explained. "Her friend called me and told me she was hurt."

"Oh my Lord. Well, do they know what's wrong?" she questioned.

"Ion know." I sighed. "That's why I'm on the way to the hospital."

"Boy don't get fresh with me," she fussed. "You better be glad she forgave your little raggedy behind. You better take care of her too."

"Ma who said we was together?"

"You ain't apologized to her yet?" she stressed.

I just stayed quiet. I wasn't about to get into this with her.

"I swear Remy you are a walking replica of your father," she sighed. "You mess up, you know you messed up, but you don't want to swallow your pride and make it right. You just expect her to take you back with open arms."

"Ma—" I moaned.

"Don't ma, me," she cut me off. "You sat there and told me about how you cared about her. And I know you do because you haven't even mentioned anybody since Nikki. Now I'm telling you, you betta apologize and get her back. Don't be like your daddy. Trust me, he paid for his mess for the rest of his life."

Thank God I was pulling up to the hospital. I was not in the mood for another sermon.

"Ma look, I'm sorry but I gotta go. I'm pulling up to the hospital."

I rushed and hung up the phone. She was about to go in and I wasn't trying to hear it. I walked in and searched for the waiting room where I found Tierra sitting. Her face was puffy and she looked nervous. She saw me and jumped up, running over.

"They said her neighbor found her at the bottom of the stairs. She was bleeding from her head. She lost a lot of blood," she started talking.

"What?" I asked my heart racing.

"I don't know," she sniffed. "They're not telling me much and I don't know what's going on and she's not waking up."

She started crying hard as hell and I hugged her trying to calm her down.

"Just try to calm down. I'ma find out what's going on." I told her. "Here, sit down."

I walked her back to the seats and she sat down wiping her eyes. I walked back over to the receptionist area to see what I could find out and hoped to God she was okay.

SKYY PEARSON

"Skyy hurry up. You're gonna be late to school. Come on now, I want you to get there on time so you can eat breakfast."

"Okay mama." I hurried. "But I don't want to leave you here by yourself."

"Skyy who is the mama? Me or you? I will be fine. I just need you to do what I asked you to do okay? Don't worry about me baby. I'm just gonna go downtown today and see if I can get some help to get the power cut back on. I promise I'll be fine."

I looked at my mama. I could tell that she was trying to be brave but I don't even think she believed what she was saying. She wasn't fine. Things hadn't been fine in a while. She didn't think I knew, but I knew she was using. I could tell she had the itch. I had seen it with some of my friends people. She was always walking around scratching and sniffing. I was only a sixth grader but I knew what was what.

"I love you mama." I said giving her a hug.

She squeezed me and kissed the top of my head.

"I love you too baby girl," she whispered holding me a bit longer. "Now hurry up and get out to the bus stop and I will see you when you get home okay?"

"Okay." I nodded.

I left and ran to the bus stop. I was hungry. Money had been tight since *my mother started using. It wasn't really any food in the house like that. Of course, she was getting money from Social Security but I never saw any of it. I wasn't going to say anything either. I was a child. I didn't want to make her mad or make her feel guilty. I just wanted her to get better.*

I got on the bus and my friend Lauren sat down next to me.

"Hey girl," she greeted.

"Hey." I yawned.

"I got something for you."

She pulled a brown paper bag out of her backpack. I opened it and saw it was some granola bars and an apple.

"I figured you'd be hungry," she told me with a small smile.

"Thanks." I said stuffing it in my backpack before anybody could notice.

I didn't want anybody in my business talking about me. I yawned again realizing how tired I was. I listened to Lauren talk about what was happening with her brother and how he was getting in trouble for slanging on the block. All I wanted to do was sleep. Mama didn't think I knew but when I went to bed I heard her leave. I knew that she wasn't staying in the house. I don't know where she was going and it kept me up all hours of the night worried.

I leaned against the window of the bus and dozed off.

"Skyy. Skyy please wake up. Skyy please, I swear I can't take this please get up."

"Hmmm?"

"Oh my God she's awake! Oh thank God!"

I opened my eyes and looked around. I could hear Tierra's voice but I couldn't see her until she came running up to the bed.

"Ma'am, I need you to take a step back for a minute," a young black girl said stepping towards me.

I wasn't on the school bus. Where the hell was I?

The more that I looked around and the more that I focused, I realize that I was at the hospital.

"Wh—wh—what happened?"

"Ms. Pearson, I'm your nurse, Simone," she told me. "I'm going to go get the doctor for you okay? Just try to relax."

She rushed out of my room and I laid there confused. I couldn't feel my leg so I tried to move it but nothing was happening. Oh shit! My leg was broken. It all started coming back to me.

"T—"

"Yea?" she replied.

"Are you okay?"

She laughed and wiped her eyes.

"Skyy, you scared the shit out of us. Oh my God, I'm so glad you're okay," she sighed.

The nurse came back in with the doctor and everybody was standing over me.

"I'm sorry ma'am but we have to ask you to step out for a moment so that we can examine Ms. Pearson," the nurse told her.

"Okay." Tierra agreed. "Skyy I'm gonna step outside."

I nodded and tried to sit up. I listened as the doctor started talking and I was just completely floored. Apparently, Malachi had left my ass on the ground to die. If the neighbor hadn't found me I might've bled out. My left leg was broken from the fall and they were monitoring me from the concussion. I couldn't believe this. He left me to die?

They spent almost twenty minutes running tests and everything before they were assured that I was okay. Tierra came back in and I felt better but I was tired.

"Where is she? Why the hell didn't y'all come get me like I said!" I heard.

"What in the world is going on?" I strained.

"Sir, I'm sorry but only one family member at a time can be back there," a second nurse tried to explain.

"Yea well, try to stop me."

I recognized the voice the closer that he got. Remy came bursting through the door and we all looked in his direction.

"Sir, you need to leave," the doctor announced.

"The hell I am. That's my girl," he snapped.

I was shocked to see him there after he showed up to my place. I never expected to see him again.

"Ms.Pearson, are you okay with him being here?" the nurse asked. "Do we need to get security?"

"Man if you don't get the fuck—"

"I'm fine." I said cutting Remy off. "I just...I need a minute. Please."

The doctor looked at the nurse and at Remy. I think everybody in the room knew that the only way Remy was leaving the room was in cuffs, and even then, he wasn't going down easy.

"We can give you a few minutes. But you need to get your rest," the doctor told me.

I nodded in understanding and the two left leaving Remy and Tierra in the room.

"What happened? Are you okay?" Remy asked as soon as they left.

"Why do you care?" I said. "Shouldn't you be with your baby mama right now doing Lamaze or something?"

He looked at me and narrowed his eyes.

"What the fu—yo are you serious?"

"Skyy don't start this shit." Tierra warned. "Obviously he cares because he's here. He's been here for the last two days while you were unconscious. He hasn't left."

"You called him?" I asked.

"Yes!" she stressed. "Yes I did. Your hard headed ass needs him. Skyy what else is it going to take for you to just let go of the dumb shit?"

I don't know why but I started tearing up. Fuck. I was trying to hold it together but I guess all these weeks of loneliness, pain, and hurt just poured out and I started bawling like a baby.

Remy came over and grabbed my hand, squeezing it tight.

"Skyy baby I'm sorry about not telling you about the baby," he apologized again. "I just didn't want to say shit because I didn't know if it was mine or not. Yeah I was fucking with her before we met. And yeah a few times before me and you really got tight. I know that was fucked up. I didn't think me and you would end up together but baby I promise you I'm glad that we did. Because I love you. I don't want her. I want you."

"You hurt me so bad Remy." I cried. "It hurt me so bad when she told me. I thought you were doing me like Malachi did."

"I know baby," he whispered rubbing my head. "But baby you

know I ain't that nigga. I fucked up. And if I got to fight to prove I ain't that nigga, I will."

I nodded and sniffed.

"I can't believe he did this to me." I said wiping my eyes.

Remy stood up and his face turned hard. Tierra looked up at me from the corner of the room she had sat in.

"What you mean he did this to you?" he asked.

I took a deep breath and started to explain.

"When you left, Malachi came in and started talking about getting back together. I was kind of thrown when he showed up."

"Wait, Malachi was at your house?" Tierra asked.

"Yea." I nodded.

"How did he know where you lived?"

"He told me that he hired a private investigator and that they had been following me around for a couple of weeks since he saw us at the restaurant that day." I told her. "He said that he knew where I lived, where I worked, and that I even enrolled in school. I got pissed off and we started arguing. Shit just blew up. He told me that he cheated and I told him that he needed to get the hell out. And then the next thing I know, he's literally on his knees begging me for my forgiveness. He then grabs me, pulls me down and causes me to fall down the stairs. I don't know if he meant to do it, but he took off and left me there."

Tierra's mouth dropped open and Remy's jaw was tight.

"So this nigga was following you and pushed you down some fucking stairs?" he gritted. "Is that what you're telling me?"

I nodded and wiped the tears that started to fall again.

"I don't think he did it on purpose though." I said. "I don't know. I just remember him standing over me and then I blacked out."

His fists were balled up tight and both him and Tierra looked furious.

"Remy, whatever you're thinking, don't okay?" I said. "The cops are already going to handle it."

"Nah," he shook his head.

"No Skyy. That nigga need to pay." Tierra spoke. "I'm sick of this muthafucka."

"I know." I agreed. "But I just don't want y'all to do anything right now. Because if you go after him, I'm sure that he will get his family involved. He'll have everybody in the state of fucking North Carolina coming after you. And you don't need that shit. Not right now."

"I don't give a fuck about who that bitch ass muthafucka can get to come after me!" he spat punching the wall. "He coulda killed you!"

"Remy please!" I cried. "Please just stop!"

My whole body was shaking as he continued to yell and go off. If one of the nurses called security up here there was no doubt that they would try to restrain him somehow and call the police. That's the last thing I needed right now.

"Babe please." I begged.

"I swear that nigga gone see me," he promised. "Oh, he gone see me for real."

I knew that it was nothing I could do to stop him. Remy had a look on his face that I had never seen before.

"Remy can you just—hold me?" I whispered.

He calmed down and walked back over to me pulling a chair next to the bed.

"Baby I'm sorry," he repeated. "If I hadn't of left and checked his ass earlier, this shit probably would've never happened. But it ain't gonna happen again understand? I got you. Don't worry about shit else. I got you baby."

He kissed me and I felt better. I knew that he wouldn't hurt me and I knew that he wasn't Malachi. Remy was a man. He was my man. And I'd be damned if I let another bitch have him.

REMY

"Woman will you be still? You not gonna get better any faster if you don't sit the fuck down."

"Will you stop fussing at me like I'm four years old?" she whined. "Remy I'm fine. It's good that I'm moving about like this."

"Yeah okay." I said shaking my head as Skyy hobbled over to the bed.

She had just gotten out of the shower and was sitting down to put her lotion on. I was sitting on the bed looking through my phone. Dymond had called my phone but I didn't answer it. She had called me twice that morning. I was enjoying my time with Skyy and didn't want to fuck up the mood with her. The minute I talked to Dymond I knew it would be nothing but drama.

I was trying to make sure that Skyy was good. She was staying with me since she had been discharged from the hospital. She was supposed to be relaxing, but here she was bopping around like she hadn't broke her leg a month ago. She needed to sit her ass down somewhere otherwise I was going to treat her like that girl did in the movie Misery.

"What time y'all leaving for Florida tomorrow?" she asked getting situated on the bed.

"I'm not. Dre gone handle that for me." I told her.

"What?" she said turning and looking at me. "You gone let Dre handle it? The nigga that don't know how to talk to people? The nigga that get into it with like everybody?"

"He knows what to do." I said. "I'm chillin."

"Remy," she sighed, turning her body to lay down. "Baby it's just a broken leg. It's healing. A lot better than what you did to Malachi by the way."

"I mean...all I can say is that nigga deserved it." I shrugged.

"Well don't you think that's something that I should've decided on? I mean, don't get me wrong, what he did was fucked up. But y'all fucking him up like that?"

"Why are you sitting here defending that nigga?" I asked confused.

"I'm not!" she argued. "I'm just saying. I know that he didn't do it on purpose. The fucked up part was when he left me sitting there. He should've gotten help. I agree with you on that. I mean, I did almost die. But, he's left me alone since then. Although I can't blame him considering you broke BOTH of his legs."

"Well you know what the Bible says, an eye for an eye right?" I teased.

She shook her head and smirked.

"How is it that I have a boyfriend that's in the streets and that goes to church?" She laughed.

"Have you met my mama?" I reminded her.

"True," she nodded as we both laughed.

I leaned over and helped her prop her leg up and laid down next to her. She may have thought I was joking but I meant what I said. I wanted to body that nigga. For her to be in the hospital and be unconscious for almost two days was scary as fuck to me. I hadn't felt that kind of fear since I lost my pops as a kid. I had lost a lot of homies and niggas on the squad, but when it's somebody that you love? The shit hit different.

Shit was going good with me and Skyy now though. After all the petty ass arguments and ignoring each other, we got back together. Shit was crazy the first couple of weeks because cops came sniffing around talking about my connection with that fuck nigga getting fucked up. She was worried that he would try to press charges but I knew he never would. He had left her to die so I knew his guilty ass wouldn't do shit. Not after knowing how bad she had been hurt because of him. He knew what he did and he deserved what he got.

I wasn't sorry for a damn thing. The only thing that I was remotely sorry for was that I couldn't completely bury his ass. But as long as Skyy was good then I was cool.

I got closer to her grabbing her and holding her tight. It had been about a month since everything happened, and we were back like never before. We were together every day. She had met my mother who managed to drag both of us to church. Of course my mother was elated and telling everybody how I was in love and everything. Now every time I talked to my mama, she was calling Skyy her daughter. Everything was good.

For the first time in a long time your boy was happy and it wasn't because of money or none of that shit. This was just that goofy eyed, hearts and flowers, in love type shit. Everything was perfect. Well almost everything. I had one fucking problem; Dymond.

She was calling all the time acting like I had broken up with her or something. Texting me how she missed me and all that shit. I had told Skyy about me fucking her while we broke up. She wasn't happy about it but she didn't trip on me. I was with her now.

"So what time are you leaving for Florida tomorrow?" She repeated.

"Yo, you hardheaded." I said. "I told you I'm not going to Florida. I'm not about to leave you here. What if something happens?"

"Something like what?" she questioned. "Rem I get around all day every day like it's nothing. And worse case if I really need something, I can just call Tierra. She around more now for Dante ass."

"Yo, what's going on with them two?" I asked her.

"They been chilling for a minute," she told me. "They started talking a while back but it looks like they're pretty serious now."

"Damn. That's wassup." I nodded seeing another call coming in from Dymond. "He seems to like her and shit."

"Yea. She definitely likes him. I haven't really seen her talking to nobody else so he must be doing something to keep her attention. But stop trying to change the subject. Negro you need to go to Florida and handle business," she fussed.

"Woman, don't worry about me." I said.

"Nope. That's not how that goes. Isn't a queen supposed to have her kings back?" She purred looking at me.

I grinned and kissed her.

"You right babe." I smiled. "Did I ever tell you how much I love you?"

"Mmm don't tell me. Show me," she cooed.

"Oh I plan on it. And I know you can't run?" I grinned devilishly.

"Who said I was going to run?" she challenged.

"Aight." I said sitting up. "You gone write a check that your pussy can't cash."

"Whatever," she giggled.

I jumped up and got in between her legs quick. She squealed, knowing that I was about to take her ass out.

"Damn it's so much that I want to do to you." I said looking into those pretty eyes of hers. "I wanna flip your ass over right now and fuck you til you go numb. But lucky for you, I can't. That still doesn't mean that I ain't gon take it out on that pussy. The way I'm gonna eat, I promise you that your soul is gonna leave your body and give you high fives."

Her eyes got big because she knew I would do it too. She was basically helpless laying there in a T-shirt. I raised it up so I could get access to her pussy and started making my way up her thighs smiling at her.

"Damn this motherfucker pretty." I admired before diving in.

She started squirming the more I licked and sucked on her pearl. I knew that she loved it whenever I did that shit. I slid my fingers into her pussy and started to finger fuck her while I ate her out.

"Oooh sh—sh—shit!" she stammered.

She was shaking and convulsing and a nigga was loving it. I watched her get pleasure as I kept fingering and licking her pussy.

"Fuck! Remy!" she cried out. "Ooh baby I love the way you eat my pussy!"

I responded to her by simply speeding up and making her grip the covers between her fingers.

"S—S—slow down baby!" she begged. "You know you bout to make me cum! Oh shit!"

I could feel her juices start to drip and I caught all of it.

"Oh my fuckin God!" she screamed. "Shhhhat!"

I took my tongue and pushed her legs back slightly so that I could lick her from her pussy to her ass. I heard her gasp and she couldn't even scream. Yeah, a nigga was eating the booty. I knew she would like that shit.

I heard my phone ring again and I knew that it was Dymond's ass. I really wished that she would stop fucking calling me. Neither one of us was given a fuck about the cell phone right then though.

I finished tasting her after she came a few more times and my dick was hard as hell. I was ready to invade her walls and fill her womb.

I took my clothes off slow and made sure to take it easy getting in between her legs. I wanted to do a whole lot of things to her. I wanted her to run. I wanted to fuck her from the back. But considering her leg, we were kind of limited.

I eased inside of her and she hissed adjusting to my size.

"Damn you tight as fuck." I observed.

Every time I fucked Skyy, it felt like heaven. She was always so tight. It would open up for me and swallow my dick.

"Shit." I mumbled enjoying the sensation.

I stroked her slow and looked at her making sure she was good.

"Baby that dick feel so good," she purred.

"Oh yea?" I grinned pulling the choke and stroke on her.

She moaned and I squeezed lightly around her neck making her heave while I dug deeper. I took my other hand and massaged her titties lifting her shirt up so that I could pop one of them in my mouth. She whimpered enjoying how good it felt.

Her pussy was gripping my dick tight. It was hard to hold on.

"Damn I love you girl." I said.

"I love you too baby," she whispered.

I quickly covered her mouth kissing her hard and explored her mouth with mine. She moaned against my lips and I knew that I was about to bust. I started to speed up and she gripped her nails in my back digging deep, screaming my name.

"Shit I'm bout to nut" I told her.

"Oooh yes daddy. Cum for me baby," she cried out.

Anytime we had fucked before, I would pull out but that shit didn't happen today. The shit was feeling too good and the way she was squeezing my dick with her pussy there was no way in hell I was coming up out of here.

"Fuck!" I grunted. I collapsed on her body and took a few seconds to get it together. "Shit." I said pulling out.

Both of us were trying to catch our breath and I got up to get a towel for her. She sat up and I cleaned her off.

"You good?" I asked.

"Yea," she sighed smiling.

I walked over to the nightstand and picked up my phone. Dymond had texted me, and I already knew the minute I opened it, it was about to be some bullshit.

"You need to tell them niggas to try to leave you alone for a bit," she fussed.

"Uh…these ain't my boys." I said frowning. "It's Dymond."

She got quiet and looked at me.

"Mmm. What does she want?"

"She's in labor." I told her reading the text message.

"How the fuck is she in labor if she's only like seven months?" She asked.

"I don't know." I said. "But, I need to go find out what's going on."

"So like she's legit in labor?"

"Yea." I said turning my phone around to show her the text.

Thank God I had been deleting the messages as they were coming in. I didn't want to give Skyy any reason to go off. Dymond was always messaging me on some dumb shit but now she was actually in labor. I knew she was hella early.

169

"I guess you gotta go handle your business then," she mumbled.

Attitude was bouncing all over her. She wasn't happy about this shit. Which meant I wasn't going to be happy about shit.

"Babe come on, you know it ain't like that." I tried to explain. "I just got to go see what's going on. What, do you want me to call her?"

"Yeah," she said folding her arms and looking at me.

"Okay." I nodded.

I called Dymond's phone and a voice I had never heard before answered.

"Hello?"

"Yea uh...Dymond there?"

"We're at the hospital. She's in early preterm labor," they said. "They've got her in a room."

"All right. I'll be there." I could hear beeping and machines in the background so I assumed that she was at the hospital. I hung up the phone and looked at Skyy who still didn't seem any less bothered.

"See? I'm telling the truth."

"Yeah I know," she sighed rolling her eyes and picking up the remote control to turn on the TV.

"I promise, I'm a go check on her that's it. It ain't no other shit, you know that."

"I know," she admitted. "But she doesn't seem to care. I'm not gon lie and say that I'm cool with this shit. I mean hell, this is pretty much life-changing."

"I know." I agreed. "But babe, I can't just bail on her either, especially if the baby is mine."

"And if it is yours then that means that I have to deal with her and her petty ass bullshit for the rest of my life. That's not fair to me," she argued.

"I never said that it was!" I could tell this shit was leading to an argument so I calmed down. "Baby, I'm not trying to argue with you. I'm just trying to do the right thing."

"The right thing would've been to wear a damn condom when you fucked her ass," she hissed. "But whatever. I know you got to be there for her. So, just go make sure she's good I guess. But Remy, I'm telling you, if she's still on that dumb shit, I don't care if she's pregnant or not. I will drag that hoe."

"I know babe." I said walking over to her and giving her a kiss. "I promise, ain't gon be no bullshit. Especially from me."

"Okay," she nodded turning the TV on.

I threw some clothes on and headed out the door. I knew this shit was about to be a whole lot more difficult once Dymond had this baby if it was mine.

I headed to the hospital thinking about how the hell I was going to deal with this shit. I love Skyy. I love the fuck out of her. But I knew this shit wasn't fair to her. I damn sure didn't want to be with Dymond. I didn't want to have anything to do with her. But I didn't have a clue how the fuck I was going to handle my responsibilities and still be good with Skyy. I know I may have sounded like an asshole, but I really didn't want this baby to be mine. It would make my life so much easier.

I pulled up to the hospital and tried to figure out how I was going to pretend that I was cool with this shit. After waiting for almost ten minutes, they took me to the room Dymond had been admitted to and she was looking scared as hell. She was hooked up to all of these monitors, and was crying hard. She was in there by herself so I'm assuming either her friend had left or just stepped out for a second.

"Remy!" she cried. "They're saying the baby is coming now. I'm scared Remy."

I walked over to her and she reached for my hand. I was being an asshole because I was hoping like hell that I could be anywhere in the world but here right now. But, I created this shit.

"I'm here." I told her.

"I called you and I called," she cried.

The door opened and in walked the doctor.

"Well, we ran a few tests but it doesn't look like the medicine is working to slow the labor down," he informed us. "The babies heart rate is dropping tremendously so we're going to have to do an emergency C-section."

"What?" She asked in a panic. "But what about just a regular delivery?"

"I'm sorry but I fear that if we try to just go ahead and induce labor, that the baby could die," he said.

Her eyes started watering up and she looked at me. I honestly didn't know what to say.

"What we're gonna do is go ahead and get you prepped," he instructed. "The good thing is, a lot of babies now are surviving despite being born this early. The bad thing is the babies lungs may not be fully developed yet so that is why we want to do the C-section immediately okay?"

"Okay," she sniffed.

Tears were streaming down her face and the doctor handed her some tissue. He looked at me standing there emotionless like I wasn't shit for not comforting her.

"All right, I'll go get everything set up," he announced. "See you in a few minutes."

He left and she turned to me.

"Why is this happening? Why is the baby coming early? They're saying that the baby may not be okay? I didn't do anything wrong. Remy why is all this happening? What am I gonna do? I'm so scared right now."

"I know." I nodded. "It's gonna be okay." I told her.

I didn't know if the shit was actually true. I didn't know what the fuck was going to happen. I had never been in this situation before. But it just seemed like the right thing to say. I just wished I believed that shit myself.

SKYY

"Hey girl. What you doing?"

"Nothing. About to go grab something to eat with Dante in a little bit before he gets ready to leave. What's up? You okay?"

"Yea I'm cool." I told her. "Just sitting here at the house."

"Where is Remy?" she asked.

"He just left." I said. "Girl get this. Apparently Dymond's ass just went into labor."

"Oh word?" she said. "Damn. You need me to come over?"

"Nah it's okay." I said. "Go ahead and do your thing with Dante."

"Girl no it's cool," she argued. "I can be there in about twenty minutes."

"No T. I don't wanna mess up your plans with your man. I know they about to be out of town, so I'm sure you probably wanna spend some time with him." I sighed dramatically.

"Girl you are fine," she replied. "So get your crippled ass dressed and we can go out. Now are you at your house or are you at Remy's?"

"I'm at Remy's." I told her.

"Alright. I'll be there soon. Just go ahead and leave the door unlocked because I know it's gonna take you a minute to get there."

"Okay." I laughed.

I hung up the phone and took my time getting out of the bed. I needed to take another shower and get dressed. I knew it would take me a minute since I was still crippled. Getting out of the house would be good. Otherwise I would start thinking about that bitch and my man. Just the thought of Remy being there with Dymond sickened me.

I hated that bitch. Since the day I met her she has been the bane of my existence. She was worse than Malachi's ass. I was trying not to think about it, but it was hard. What if this baby was his? Why the fuck was she in labor all of a sudden? Knowing her, she probably did some shit when she found out we got back together to make her ass go into early labor. I know it sounds wrong, but I wouldn't put shit past her. She would do anything to get Remy.

I moved as fast as I could to finish my shower and got out so that I could finish getting ready. I knew that Tierra would be pulling up soon.

About five minutes later, I heard the front door beep and she called out letting me know that she was here.

"I'm in the bedroom!" I called out.

She walked to the bedroom and tossed her purse in the corner.

"What's going on girl?" she greeted. "You good?"

"Yeah I guess." I huffed. "I'm just...agitated. This shit with Dymond."

"Girl I'm so sick of hearing that name," she stressed sitting down on the bed.

"How you think I feel?" I pointed out. "I know it sounds fucked up but I really hate that bitch. Like I really hate the fact that Remy fucked this girl and didn't think to use a damn condom. Like I'm really hoping that it's not his kid because I don't want to deal with her."

"I get it," she said. "I didn't know she was that far along."

"She's not. She went into early labor." I said rolling my eyes.

"Damn. Well, I hope everything works out." I looked at her confused and she smirked. "Come on Skyy. It's not like the baby did anything wrong."

I rubbed my head and nodded.

"I know. But T this whole situation is so messed up. Like what if this baby is his? Every time I turn around she's going to be calling." I thought out loud. "Then I have to look at the baby and have a constant reminder of what they did? And you know she's going to use that baby every chance that she gets to get Remy to come around."

"Well yeah. But, you know Remy ain't gone fall for the shit," she pointed out.

"Do I?"

She shook her head and started smiling at something she was reading on her phone.

"Let me guess, Dante?" I questioned.

"Yeah," she cooed. "He's getting ready for that trip to Florida."

"Yeah I know." I said. "Remy told me that he was staying here to take care of me. But clearly that's not gonna happen since ole girl is having this damn baby."

"Alright soooo we're not gonna talk about that anymore. Let's talk about getting you out of this house!" she announced. "I need you to hurry along and get your little boot on so that you can hobble on out of here. We're gonna go eat and do a little bit of shopping and then maybe you can relax."

"I doubt it but okay." I agreed.

Tierra helped me finish getting ready and we got in the car. I sent Remy a quick text message letting him know that I was going out to lunch with my best friend. He responded with a picture of him in scrub gear and his face covered.

"Tuh." I grunted.

"What's up?" she asked turning onto a street and cutting the air on.

Even though it was December, it was extremely hot for some reason.

"He just sent me this picture." I said turning it to her so she could see.

"Well I guess it's about to go down," she replied.

I sent him a message back trying to find out an update.

Skyy: What's happening?

Bae: She has to have an emergency C-section because the baby's heart rate is dropping. We're getting ready to go in now.

Skyy: OK.

Bae: I love you.

I looked at the message and thought about whether or not I wanted to respond. I did love him. So did Dymond. But he was mine.

Skyy: I love you too. I'll see you soon.

I put my phone down and shook this shit off. I had to change my outlook on this shit. I was letting her get into my head once again, but that bitch didn't have him. I did.

"I gotta stop to get some gas real quick." Tierra told me.

"Okay."

We pulled into the gas station and she hopped out to run inside to pay. I was sitting there in the car looking around when something caught my attention. It was a couple kissing across the street. The guy looked really familiar.

"Remy?" I whispered. I strained to look because they were far away. "What the fuck?"

Tierra came back out and started to pump her gas.

"T." I called out.

"What's up?" She said.

I got out and hobbled over to where she was standing.

"Look over there." I pointed.

"Where?" She followed my gaze and squinted. "What, some nigga kissing on some chick?"

"Look close." I pressed. "Who does that look like to you?"

She stared for a few more seconds before her mouth dropped open.

"Oh shit! That's—"

"Yeah. Remy." I finished. "All up on another bitch."

To Be Continued...

Blake Karrington Presents is now accepting manuscripts from aspiring or experienced urban romance authors!

If you'd like to join the BKP family, send us the first 15K words (60 pages) of your completed manuscript to blakekarringtonpresents-books@gmail.com

Blake Karrington Presents is now accepting manuscripts from aspiring or experienced urban romance authors!

WHAT MAY PLACE YOU ABOVE THE REST:

Heroes who are the ultimate book bae: strong-willed, maybe a little rough around the edges but willing to risk it all for the woman he loves.

Heroines who are the ultimate match: the girl next door type, not perfect - has her faults but is still a decent person. One who is willing to risk it all for the man she loves.

The rest is up to you! Just be creative, think out of the box, keep it sexy and intriguing!

If you'd like to join the BKP family, send us the first 15K words (60 pages) of your completed manuscript to blakekarringtonpresentsbooks@gmail.com

Be sure to LIKE our Blake Karrington Presents page on Facebook!

LIKE OUR PAGE!

CPSIA information can be obtained
at www.ICGtesting.com
Printed in the USA
LVHW042008011020
667692LV00005B/1113